Caged

Where Most Husbands Should Be ...
for a While

H. Lena Jones

PublishAmerica
Baltimore

First printing

ISBN: 1-4137-5760-X
PUBLISHED BY PUBLISHAMERICA, LLLP
www.publishamerica.com
Baltimore

Printed in the United States of America

This book is fondly dedicated to my husband, Cy.

I thank my sister Holly and my friend Monica for their encouragements. I thank my sister-in-law Yvette for taking the time to edit my manuscript.

Prologue

Deep in the heart of the South Pacific is an island called Edengardenia. Many have heard stories of this island paradise, but no one knows exactly where it is or who was first to discover its existence.

Some have said it was Captain James Cook who first set foot on the island in 1788. Others have said it might well have been William Bligh, captain of the *Bounty*, whose crew mutinied in 1789 and set him adrift in an open boat with 18 of his loyal men. They are wrong—of that, I am certain, for there are no recorded chartings of this magnificent place!

Edengardenia is a small tropical island, nestled in luscious beauty. It is miraculously sheltered from the destructive forces of tropical storms. Flora and fauna are plentiful and add to the natural beauty of the island. In the center of this small, but magnificent island is an enormous mountain—Fijora.

It is on the summit of Fijora that a gigantic bristlecone pine tree stands. According to legend, the tree is as old as the island, for its trunk is more than two meters thick and its branches spread more than ten meters in all directions. There is a hollow at the base of the trunk. Inside this hollow is a stump large enough for a person to sit on.

The islanders have long believed some mysterious and miraculous power resides inside the hollow, for islanders will tell you that when anyone sits on the stump, a soft whisper reaches their ears, bringing them peace and happiness, which in turn, enfolds them with a special kind of warmth. The islanders refer to the tree as the

Great Pine—*the tree of solitude*. Most of the islanders regularly climb to the summit to experience this special solitude, or spiritual peacefulness.

Two paths lead to the summit and to the Great Pine. One is steep and rugged in places, but offers a breathtaking vista of the island and ocean. The other is much easier to climb, though quite long and winding with nothing of particular interest to see. This second path is rarely used.

At the base of the mountain is a hut with branches of palm trees and reed intertwining to form its thatch roof. It is here Eva, a twenty-five-year-old native, lives with her lay-about husband, Adamos, who is forty-five. The other islanders live in similar huts, scattered between the mountain and the sea. The sizes of the huts vary, depending on the number of offspring. In Eva and Adamos' case, there is none, so their hut is limited to two rooms: one for sleeping and entertaining (the main room), the other for cooking. A low dining table occupies the center of the kitchen floor, and a similar table occupies one corner of the main room.

A small stream lies a short distance from this hut. Each morning, before breakfast, Eva fetches water from the stream and heats it up for her bath. She fills another tub with water to wash the dishes, and in a large pot, boils what remains for her cooking and drinking needs. She leaves a bucket of water outside the back door in case she needs to refill the tub at night.

All Edengardenians craving spiritual peacefulness have traversed the rugged path leading to the summit of Fijora. "Just a load of foolish people believing in a load of rubbish," Adamos would say impatiently to Eva. "Solitude! Bah! I have no time for such foolishness."

"And that's a pity," Eva would say.

Pity indeed! But who am I, you may be wondering. Am I the pine tree ... the mountain ... the island ... a combination of the three? Yes! I permeate all those things, for I created them. You might also be wondering if Edengardenia is a real place. Let's just say Edengardenia can be thought of as real or imaginary, depending on the similarities between the lives of the characters depicted and yours. The Great Pine, or something similar, may be the thing you choose as a stabilizer—a constant—the thing that keeps you from going over the edge, as it were, when dealing with inconsiderate husbands, for instance. Edengardenia is where this story must be set … for it is Eva and Adamos I am observing.

Eva's tender qualities of love and charity were never more evident to me than when she ascended the mountain to seek solace after her beloved rabbit, Hoppippa, suddenly expired. "Please, Great Pine," she wept, "will you make my Hoppy live again?"

"This I mustn't do, child. Your rabbit has lived its given life and now it is time for him to rest. Perhaps you will find another," I answered.

"No! No other rabbit will ever take the place of my Hoppippa, for I cannot love another."

"Cannot or will not, Eva?"

"Cannot … will not … what does it matter? I want my Hoppy back."

There was no consoling the child, so I cloaked her with tenderness until her crying subsided. She stirred my curiosity and emotions. She was only eight … an unselfish, caring child. I decided to bestow on her the gifts of wisdom, knowledge, and a peaceful nature.

At thirteen, Eva took to herself a husband. She fascinated me even more with her maturity and unshakeable devotion to me. And yes, with the unconditional love she continues to bestow upon her undeserving husband, Adamos.

To this day, Eva remains kind, compassionate and creative, a woman with a big heart; Adamos is oftentimes too laid back, rude, and dare I say, fat—though this must remain between us, as it is 'politically incorrect' to engage such adjectives. All the same, it should be noted that words such as short, fat, and skinny are merely adjectives describing the state of the body—the shell which houses the real 'you,' the soul.

But I digress. Unlike Adamos, Eva is steadfast in her climb up the mountain every morning without fail, for she believes her time of solitude gives her strength, courage, and confidence to deal with Adamos, while maintaining her sanity and burying a deep hurt.

Adamos also fascinates me, but not for the same reasons as Eva. Adamos is a selfish man with little patience and understanding for the needs of his wife, her friends or even her family.

Just recently, I heard Adamos say, "They tell you rubbish, Eva. They lie to you; tell you what they think you want to hear. Bah! You're foolish, Eva, to believe anything they say. I am your husband. It is I, you should believe. And I tell you, Eva, you are ugly and have little brains within the space between your ears. Without me, you are nothing. That is the truth you need to hear."

But Eva was wise in her answer. "You are the only one who thinks those thoughts, Adamos. When I'm in the presence of the Great Pine, I know I'm accepted just the way I am, so it doesn't matter what you say, for your words are untrue and unkind."

"See what I mean, Eva? You feel accepted by a tree, a tree of all things. Use the little brains you have, woman. A hunk of wood has no voice or feelings."

"I will not argue, Adamos. Climb the mountain and see for yourself. Rest a while within the solitude of the Great Pine. See what gifts are revealed for you."

"No! I will not. I don't need a tree or anyone to tell me what my capabilities are, or to show me what solitude is. You must stop this madness, Eva. Stop it at once or I'll make sure you regret the day you first climbed that stupid mountain."

Adamos is convinced no intelligent person needs this unusual solitude, especially from a tree. He thinks the islanders quite mad to risk their necks on so steep and treacherous a climb. "Solitude is what I get when Eva wastes her precious time helping people, leaving me to my own devices," he mutters to himself. "Foolish woman, the meat she brings home, she never gets to enjoy, because I eat it first. I tell her the heat of the day ruined it and I had to dispose of it. Serves her right for being so gullible. Solitude! Only I know what real solitude is—ignoring Eva when she tries to tell me about her day; insulting Eva when she tells me about her friends; watching her cringe when I yell at her for no reason.

"How I detest when she tells me about those mysterious yellow nuggets she keeps finding; only she never tells me where she finds them. 'They're a blessing, Adamos, a reward for my good deeds. They build my self-confidence.'" He mockingly mimics Eva's voice. "She must have hundreds of them stored in the base of the table ... hundreds!

"And how foolish telling me how fortunate she is to be so blessed. I will one day strip her of her precious nuggets and see how blessed and self-confident she feels then. Yes, she will seek solace from the tree, but will find none. I will laugh when she discovers solace doesn't exist, unless she creates it for herself. Ah, Eva, you and the rest of our people are so foolish," concludes Adamos.

Yesterday, while Adamos was engaged in gnawing greedily on a chunk of ham bone, Eva asked him if he knew how the island came into existence. That in itself was not bad, but Eva, a woman with multiple thoughts, spewed several questions in rapid succession. One would have thought she had fired an automatic weapon, for Adamos, in a state of confusion as to which question he should answer first, choked on the bone, passed wind, and floundered about as he tried to retrieve the ham bone which had torpedoed into the air. In the end, he answered none of Eva's questions, but glared at her as a maimed bull glares at its matador.

"It's on account of the missing rib," teased Eva.

"What's on account of the rib?" demanded Adamos.

"That you cannot think of, nor do, more than one thing at a time; that my many questions confuse you."

"Don't be stupid, Eva. You talk such nonsense. It is you who are confused for not knowing which question you want answered first."

Tut! Tut!

But I digress ... again! While crime and punishment is unheard of on this magnificent island, trouble is afoot for Adamos as he makes one last attempt to crush Eva's spirit. Will he succeed? Will he follow through with his plan to strip Eva of her nuggets and ultimately destroy her self-confidence?

Come ... a new workday begins for Eva. Let us listen in on her and Adamos' conversation as they finish breakfast....

One

"Time draws near for me to start my day, Adamos. Many of our people need my help."

"It isn't them you should be fussing over, Eva, but me." Adamos stabs his thumb into his chest; his blue-green eyes still red with sleep glare at his wife.

Eva swallows the last of her scant breakfast of seagulls' eggs and crushed black beans. "Why is that?" she asks, as she puts on her hat and adds a pair of stone-sharpened whalebone scissors to the bag of tools she will need for her day of voluntary work.

"I'm the one you should be helping. I'm your husband and today I don't feel well." Adamos rubs his temples, feigning a headache.

"And what is wrong with you this time, Adamos?"

"It isn't your place to question the state of my wellness, Eva. If I say I'm sick today, then I'm sick today. I order you to stay home and take care of me."

"Sick, Adamos?" Eva conceals a smile. "It's all in your head. Get over it. That's what you tell me." She narrows her eyelids, partly concealing her gray eyes.

"Don't nag, Eva, your nagging distresses me."

"Then it's better that I should be gone all day than be the cause of further distress, my dear."

"Precisely what I expected ... no sympathy, even when I'm sick. You care more about cleaning out dung and planting cassava roots than you care about your sick husband. Ungrateful, that's what you are."

Undaunted by Adamos' latest ailment—whether real or imagined—and his constant accusations, Eva knows arguing is pointless. To fire insults at Adamos or even chastise him for his hurtful, ugly words will only bring her down to his level. Eva has long since realized Adamos no longer has any love or respect for her, but

13

it is her belief that once chosen, a husband is a lifelong commitment. She must honor that.

"If you feel well enough later, you might like to patch the roof," she suggests, ignoring Adamos' pitiful groans.

"Nag, nag, nag! You sound like a flipping parrot. I'll fix the roof when I'm good and ready, not when you say I should."

"You've been saying that for many months now, Adamos ...."

"And I'll continue saying it for as long as I please."

"Precisely what I expected to hear." Eva hides a smile with a pretend cough. Then just before she leaves, she bends her head to peck Adamos lovingly on his cheek.

"Get off, Eva. Hop it." Adamos squirms, swinging his fat arm just enough to bat her head carelessly aside. He leans his body away, causing Eva to stumble. Her length of jet-black hair comes free and her hat tumbles off her head. "If you showed me more gratitude for being your husband," continues Adamos, "and for preparing your evening meal, even when I'm sick, perhaps then I would return your pathetic attempts at affection."

Eva regains her equilibrium. She rewraps her hair into a loose bun at the nape of her neck as she says, "But you don't prepare any meals, Adamos, not anymore." She retrieves her hat from the ground, smoothing out the dent in the crown. "Most days I bring food already cooked from those whom I help ... and just as well. It saves me having to cook after a long day's work. You merely sit and wait for me to dish yours out and hand it to you as if you were the great Kahuna of Edengardenia and I was your ...."

"Whatever!" interrupts Adamos red-faced, his cheeks puff like a toad. "And why do you have to leave at the crack of dawn every day, disturbing my rest?"

"You know why, Adamos. You know I like to climb Fijora and sit in the hallowed-out trunk of the Great Pine for my share of solitude, before I start my day."

"You stupid woman, how many more times do I have drum into your thick skull that the pine is only a tree? What solitude can you get from a flaming tree, eh?"

"My dear, I've been climbing up the mountain every day since I was eight. I have no intention of stopping."

"But why, Eva? It makes no sense to me."

"Perhaps you should shift yourself up the mountain and find out what the Great Pine has for you," replies Eva softly, twirling her hat between her fingers. "I'll still be climbing the mountain if I live to be a hundred."

"I don't give a damn what you say, Eva. You won't find me doing a stupid thing like sitting in a hallowed-out tree trunk, talking to a hunk of old dead wood," says Adamos, clasping his fingers across his chest.

"Suit yourself." Eva sets the hat on her head again.

"And those yellow nuggets you keep finding. Eva, they're worthless, yet you tell me they build your self-confidence. How stupid can you be?"

"I cannot explain it, Adamos. But it is sufficient for me that I should feel more confident about myself because of them."

"How stupid you are to believe a thing like that." Adamos smirks. *Eva needs to be taught a lesson this night—one that will bring her to her senses,* thinks Adamos. *I'll leave and I'll take her nuggets with me.* "You will live to regret this, Eva, just you wait," warns Adamos, tightening his chunky arms across his middle.

"G'bye, Adamos, great Kahuna of Edengardenia. I will not allow you to steal my joy this day." Eva bows in mock reverence and backs slowly out of the little hut.

In spite of Adamos' unkind words, Eva knows her day will be a splendid one at the end of which she will miraculously find yet another mysterious yellow nugget stuffed under the straw mat at the front door of the hut. She has no idea who leaves them. (She has no economic use for the nuggets, since the people of Edengardenia barter for all their material needs.) But the pea-sized nuggets seem to strengthen her self-confidence and self-esteem ... and dull the pain Adamos caused one year after they were married—a pain Eva will take to her grave!

Eva stands for a moment with her back pressed against the door.

Sunlight is just breaking through the morning mist. She inhales the freshness, almost tasting its sweetness. She is looking forward to her climb to the summit, where she will sit quietly on the stump inside the hollow of the Great Pine.

Thoughts of her many visits to the Great Pine dance inside her head as she hurries down the narrow dirt path along the base of the mountain. Sometimes she wishes she had the courage to break her silence and talk about Adamos. How she wishes he were more like the loving husband she once knew, instead of the sarcastic, self-centered, arrogant fool he has become. But that is complaining, which is wrong. Eva has come to realize that whenever she complains to anyone about Adamos, she experiences a sore throat.

Eva climbs the mountain with ease and once settled in the hollow of the Great Pine, feels the solitude wrap around her like a mother cuddling her babe. She closes her eyes, enjoying the feeling of love, acceptance, and appreciation so freely given. Her heart overflows with joy. It is all she needs today.

All too soon, she knows it is time to leave. Suddenly without warning, the thoughts in her head force past her lips. The silence in the hollow shatters, like broken glass.

"Tell me, Great Pine, is it I who should change my ways like Adamos says? Shouldn't I help those in need even though it brings me much joy and fulfillment? Why can't Adamos be more supportive? Is it because of the tale our ancestors tell—that a single rib was taken from man to create woman? Is that why Adamos thinks he should be worshipped—for relinquishing one rib? Am I an ungrateful wife as Adamos says? And tell me, Great Pine, who is it that has been leaving the nuggets beneath my doormat all this time? Is it a reward for my kindness to others?"

Eva's voice is gentle but urgent. A direct answer is not one she will receive today; instead, she feels the usual tingles consuming her body, a feeling she has come to realize as an extra special hug. It feels so comforting. "Forgive me if I have been outspoken, Great Pine. I shouldn't have questioned you so, or complained about Adamos." Eva swallows, but feels no soreness in her throat.

Eva makes no attempt to leave. Instead, she allows her mind to drift back to when she was a girl of eight, when she made her first climb up the mountain to the Great Pine. She remembers how heartbroken she felt when she sat upon this very stump, crying her eyes out because her pet rabbit had died. She wanted no other rabbit to replace her beloved Hoppippa. She remembers how she felt love and tenderness enfold her, willing her not to be so sad, but to smile in the face of adversity and remain assured time is a great healer of all wounds.

She remembers that, by the time she had left the solitude of the Great Pine, she had acquired the knowledge of how to use her hands to repair broken things and how to give advice on how best to plant vegetables and cassava roots for a bountiful crop. She could not explain this wisdom, except to say the Great Pine had given her many talents and gifts in exchange for the death of her beloved rabbit.

Eva thinks of the yellow nuggets again. She always finds them under the doormat when she returns from her day of voluntary work. The first time was after a terrible argument with Adamos when he had reduced her to tears and enjoyed watching her sob. She had raced from the hut to hide her pain, but ended up helping farmer Tusslebark pick tomatoes. Finding the nugget under the mat when she returned home had restored some of her confidence and courage to face Adamos.

The second time she found a nugget was after she had fetched several buckets of shells from the beach for old Millie—the island's official historian, to make a track from her front door to the footpath leading to the mountain. The third time was when she had taken the trouble to stop and care for an old mangy dog, which the other islanders just ignored.

By now, she should have hundreds of nuggets stored in the old wooden box, which she and Adamos use as the base for the table in the main room. "Perhaps tonight I will ask Adamos to help me count the nuggets," whispers Eva. "Then maybe the desire to climb the mountain will be strong in him, for I believe it is only then that Adamos will find it in his heart to love and respect me as he used to."

Two

Back at the hut, Adamos does nothing but eat and plan Eva's punishment—his departure with her precious nuggets! It is just past noon when he begins to put his plan into action. There are no sacks in which to pile the nuggets. Finding one of his old trousers, Adamos rips it down the middle, separating the legs. He takes a length of vine and cuts it into short pieces. He uses two of the pieces to tie the bottom of each trouser leg.

Pleased with the new use for his old trousers, Adamos shifts the top off the table exposing the nuggets. Pity he will not be around to see Eva's reaction when she finds them gone. He shovels out handfuls of the nuggets with his bare hand, pouring them loosely down each trouser leg. He uses more pieces of vine to secure the opening at the top of each leg. He gives each leg a final shake to make certain no nuggets escape. Satisfied, he folds each leg in half.

"Now for a place to hide these," mutters Adamos. His greedy, gleaming eyes dart about the hut, coming to rest on his grass-stuffed mattress. "I'll dig a shallow hole in the ground beneath my mattress. That will be a perfect place to conceal the nuggets."

Dust particles dance in the steady stream of sunlight pouring through a crack in the thatched roof. Adamos eyes the opening; a smirk creases his face. "'Fix the roof, Adamos … patch the wall, Adamos … it's been months since you promised, Adamos.'" He imitates Eva's voice. "Well, I won't be fixing no blinking holes now," he says aloud. "I have other plans—plans that will humble Eva for good."

Adamos grabs an old wooden spoon from the kitchen. Kicking his mattress aside, he kneels on the hard ground and begins to scrape and dig out soil to make a shallow hole wide enough to accommodate his bundles of nuggets. Next, he buries the folded trousers legs. He backfills the hole, spreading the excess dirt evenly, before plopping the mattress back in place.

"I must make certain Eva doesn't go anywhere near her nugget collection this night," mutters Adamos, wiping sweat from his brow with the back of his hand. "I will make sure she starts another pile some place else. By the time she realizes the nuggets are missing, I'll be long gone. This very night she will be eating humble pie soaked in tears and snot."

Satisfied with the progress of his plan, Adamos returns to the kitchen and devours the last of the meat. He will clean up the mess he has made and remove all traces of the food he has eaten just before Eva returns home that evening.

Too full to move, Adamos slouches at the kitchen table, his legs spread apart to balance his large bottom squarely on the stump used for a seat. He yawns a few times, but his thoughts are focused on timing his escape. He must leave in the dead of night when Eva is asleep. This will depend on how deeply she sleeps, though. Perhaps he will put a few drops of sleepeazy bark juice into her bedtime tea—it had worked on him when he had to yank out his rotting, aching toenail. "It was the day I decided to stop working altogether!" he murmurs before turning his thoughts back to the plan at hand. Until then, he must remain awake to keep Eva away from her nuggets.

But overeating takes its toll on Adamos. His eyelids flutter and droop; sleep feels like a pleasure he must have. With some effort, he pushes away from the table and ambles into the main room. He drops onto his bed of dried grass, intending to have a few minutes of shut-eye. The fresh mound beneath his mattress pokes into the middle of his back. Adamos shifts his mattress so the mound is beneath his pillow. He resettles, appreciating the new elevation of his head. Adamos burrows beneath the warmth of two woven blankets and yawns again. "I will rest my eyes a little ... I'll count to forty, then open them. One nugget ... two nuggets ... three nugg ...!"

With a contented smile on his face, and delicious thoughts of crushing Eva, Adamos drifts into sweet slumber.

Three

It is dusk by the time Eva returns home from another satisfying day of voluntary work: two farmers needed cassava roots and carrots planted; the blacksmith needed help shoeing some of the packhorses; and her sister, Neena, suggested they build a new cage for her pet mongoose. As a reward for her help, the farmers have given Eva some vegetables and a ham from a wild boar. Her sister had offered to cook ham and vegetable stew, if Eva wanted.

"Adamos will be pleased with the ham and vegetables," Eva had said to the farmers, thanking them.

And to her sister, she had smiled and said, "Perhaps one day, I will take you up on your offer, for you are surely a better cook than I could ever be."

"Or Adamos for that matter," her sister had replied, thinking Adamos prepares meals for Eva.

"Aye! But once upon a time my Adamos was an excellent cook."

Eva lifts the straw mat at her front door and, as usual, finds a new nugget. She looks towards the mountain and mouths "thank you" before curling her fingers around the object. She will continue to think of it as her reward.

"Adamos!" she calls once she is inside the hut. She wonders why no lamps burn. "Adamos," she calls again, reaching for the flint to light the lamp just inside the front door. "Perhaps he has taken my advice and shifted his bulk up the mountain." Preoccupied with the task at hand, Eva bursts into song, seizing the opportunity of Adamos' absence to lift her voice in merriment. With the lamp in one hand and the nugget in the other, she trudges over to add the nugget to her collection.

Adamos stirs from sleep as he hears what he thinks is the distant yowling of a strangled cat in much distress. But the yowls are familiar. When the yowls break into song, Adamos comes to his senses. "Eva!

20

She's home!" He did not intend to sleep this long!

Fully awake now, Adamos spies Eva walking slowly towards the table and her store of nuggets. He eyes her shoulder bag, in which he is certain she has cooked meat from whomever she has helped that day. "Ooooooohwaaaaa!" Adamos groans softly at first, but when Eva does not react, he groans louder. "That should stir any old sleeping dragon," Adamos whispers, burying his head under the blankets.

This time Eva hears Adamos' pitiful groans and turns from the table. She shoves the nugget into her pocket. "Adamos?" she says, holding the light up so it casts its brightness around the small room, pushing the darkness to the far corners. She sees the large lump of her husband encased in blankets. "My dear," she says, her voice sorrowful. "I thought you were out, otherwise I wouldn't have burst into song, knowing how much you can't stand my singing. Are you still feeling unwell?" Eva drops her bag on the floor and hurries to kneel beside her husband. Her heart is sorrowful for not believing he was truly sick. She settles the lamp on the ground.

Adamos utters another mournful, pitiful groan. He feels hot, not because he has a fever, but because the two blankets are making him sweat. Perfect!

Eva peels back the blankets a fraction and immediately feels heat emanating from Adamos' head and face. Beads of sweat saturate his face. "You're burning up, Adamos. Have you a temperature?"

For effect, Adamos moans again. "I should hope I have a temperature, Eva, otherwise I would be dead."

"Tell me, Adamos, what can I do to break the fever?" Eva's voice is gentle. "Let me sponge your head with cold water from the stream."

Adamos stirs then. He does not wish to be drenched. "No, Eva," he whispers in a pretend hoarse voice, "just leave me be. The pounding in my head will soon stop. I'll help you prepare the meal … I don't feel hungry, though."

"Not hungry? How sick you must be to have lost your appetite. Rest, my dear, I will bring you a change of clothing, for you've sweated much."

Adamos pulls the blankets over his head. "As you wish." But in his mind he is calculating the hours to Eva's bedtime.

"At least I shan't have to cook," says Eva. "I can make use of the leftovers, for we only consumed a small portion of meat and vegetables last night."

Under the blankets, Adamos' eyes pop wide open. He has eaten all the meat ... and carrots ... and lettuce! There is nothing left for Eva. Exhibiting a pained face, squinting and flickering eyelids, Adamos lifts his head above the blankets. "I'm sorry, Eva. Maggots infested the meat ... the lettuce wilted, and the carrots shriveled. So I threw them out. There's nothing to eat, unless you brought ... did you bring ...." Adamos is in a panic. *Eva will see the dirty bowls and scraps in the kitchen and will know I have been stuffing myself.*

"Maggots?" interrupts Eva, one eyebrow arched. The meat and vegetables were fresh when she brought them home the night before. The day wasn't so hot as to cause the food to spoil. She shakes her head. She will not argue with him because he is sick. "It must have been the heat that spoilt the meat and ruined the vegetables," she agrees, convinced that Adamos has devoured the leftovers.

Leaving the lamp on the ground, Eva hurries off and lights two others. This done, she fetches Adamos a clean nightshirt and a cap to keep his head warm.

"Have you brought cooked meat, Eva?" Adamos struggles to separate himself from the blankets.

Eva does not answer, for she is already in the kitchen staring in disbelief at the soiled dishes revealing traces of the previous night's meal. She does not understand why Adamos has lied about the meat going bad. Just as well, farmer Johan has given her smoked boar meat, cassava roots, and vegetables. She will set aside some of the meat for herself before Adamos can lay his hands on it. Removing the meat from her bag, she slices off a chunk and has only just slipped it into a pot when Adamos shuffles into the kitchen, holding his head. His beady eyes zoom in on what is left of the boar's ham; his mouth waters.

"My dear," says Eva, watching him closely, "you should be resting.

Oh, you haven't even changed out of your wet things. Adamos, you will catch a chill." Behind her back, she pushes the pot containing the hefty chunk of meat out of Adamos' line of vision.

"I feel guilty leaving you to fend for yourself after such a long work day," replies Adamos in a weakened voice. How it pained him to show sympathy to Eva, but he must sustain this act. "The colored lines and flashing lights from my aching head are faint now. I'm sorry for being so sick all day. Let me fix your meal."

"But my dear," protests Eva, puzzled by Adamos' sudden concern for her, and his willingness to prepare her a meal.

"Ah, good," interrupts Adamos, "I see you have brought more carrots, lettuce, and cassava roots. Shall I make a vegetable stew?" He pretends not to see the meaty boar's ham in full view of his darting eyes.

"With chunks of boar's meat, too," says Eva. "It's uncooked."

"Boar's meat? Uncooked?" Adamos resists licking his lips. "Perhaps we'll leave the meat for tomorrow, eh? I'll have more time then to cook you a proper meat and vegetable stew ... like I used to ... just the way you like it. Vegetable stew will be sufficient for you tonight ... it will take less time to prepare ... seeing I'm still sick and all."

Eva smiles knowing that when tomorrow comes Adamos will again tell her that the meat perished because of the heat. But an idea is already brewing in her head. "Very well, my dear. I will help cut up the vegetables as soon as I've rewrapped the meat." She quickly wraps the meat in palm leaves and hands it to Adamos before he is able to see the chunk she has reserved for herself.

With sweating hands, Adamos grabs the meat from Eva. "I'll put this where it's cool." He turns and shuffles out of the kitchen, forgetting all about the vegetable stew ... and his aching head.

When Adamos does not return, Eva realizes that he really has no intentions of preparing the meal. Eva makes a quick decision: Neena will make her a nice stew. Eva fetches her large, hand-woven shoulder bag and creates a hollow big enough to conceal the pan containing the boar's meat. She will not bother to include carrots and cassava roots. She slings the bag over her shoulder and heads towards the main room, where she is certain she will find Adamos tucked under his blankets, the parcel of meat close to his head.

She is right. "My dear," says Eva in a sympathetic voice, "I must go out for a while."

"Can't it wait til morning?" asks Adamos, his large tummy pushing the blankets up and down with every labored breath. *The sooner Eva drinks her sleepeazy bark tea, the sooner he can leave.*

"I forgot to stop at Neena's to repair a broken leg on her table and mend the hole in her front door." (This, of course, is not true.)

"Can't it wait 'til tomorrow?" complains Adamos with pretend concern. But the thought of Eva away from the hut will give him enough time to boil a piece of the boar's ham and prepare a meal for himself, for he is beginning to feel hungry again. Already it feels good that he does not have to share the precious food with his wife, but he must continue to show objection. "Always helping your sister. Doesn't she have anyone else who could help her?"

"Why should she, dear, when she has such a capable sister?"

"Bah!" says Adamos, his double chin wobbling. *You capable?* he thinks mockingly. "Will you be long?"

"Not too long, I hope." Eva shuffles to the door and just before she opens it, she says over her shoulder, "When I return, Adamos, I plan to count my nuggets. I should have quite a few by now I should think."

The blankets fly back rapidly and Adamos sits up abruptly. "Count the nuggets ... tonight? You mustn't," he says with a quiver in his voice.

"I see no harm in that, do you?" Eva is puzzled by her husband's defensive reaction.

"It isn't good to count nuggets at night," says Adamos, pretending to look horrified.

"Oh? Says who?"

"Legend ... Oooooh!" Adamos mops his brow with one end of the blanket.

"Legend? What legend?" This Eva wants to hear. She has never

CAGED

heard such a ridiculous thing, especially since no one else on the island owns nuggets. When Adamos clams up, the side of his mouth begins a nervous twitch. Eva narrows her eyes with suspicion, her thoughts disturbing. Adamos' nervous twitch is not a good sign. No, she thinks, I will not entertain these thoughts. "Tell me, Adamos, please, I've never heard of this legend."

Neither has Adamos for that matter. He does not want Eva counting the nuggets because he does not intend to put them back into the box. "Don't go out this night, Eva. A nice cup of tea and a good night's sleep will replenish your energies for what awaits you tomorrow."

Eva laughs softly, for Adamos has not shown concern for her welfare in years. "What awaits me tomorrow is no different from what I faced today, Adamos. I need no tea or an early sleep."

"Ah, but you do ... you will be busy tomorrow ... I can feel it in my bones."

"You are old, Adamos. What you feel in your bones is pain. The sooner I go, the sooner I will be back," says Eva.

"Then go ... if you must. You never listen to me anyway." Adamos sighs. He needs time to think.

"I shan't be gone long." Eva backs out of the hut. She will think about the nuggets later, but right now she needs to get over to Neena's so she can turn the chunk of boar's ham into a scrumptious stew along with vegetables from her garden. Her stomach growls with anticipation.

Adamos listens to Eva's footsteps fading in the distance, before he scrambles out of bed. With Eva determined to count her nuggets, he must alter his plans. He will not replace the nuggets. They are his ... his for all the years of putting up with Eva and her foolish ways. He will leave as soon as he is able to gather all he needs. The darkness will provide enough cover to conceal his hasty departure.

Four

Hauling his mattress aside, Adamos digs and scrapes away the dirt, uncovering the bundles of nuggets he has buried. He heaves the heavy bundles from the hole, brushing off excess dirt. He shoves the dirt carelessly back into the hole, before concealing it with his mattress. Grabbing old clothes and blankets, he makes a shape to look as if he is still lying there. He drapes another blanket over the shape.

Fetching the largest of Eva's tightly woven vine baskets from the kitchen, Adamos hurriedly stuffs it with the parcel of boar meat, some carrots, and the bundles of nuggets. No room remains for extra clothing, but changing his clothes is of little concern to Adamos. He extinguishes all the lamps before sneaking out the front door of the hut.

Adamos wastes no time on sentimentalities, but hurries along the path leading away from the hut and away from the mountain. The straps of the basket stretch to maximum from the weight of the nuggets. He stops briefly to sling one pant leg of nuggets over his shoulder. With each labored step Adamos takes, one thought hammers in his head: where will he go!

"Yes, where will I go?" says Adamos to himself, turning to stare at the hut he has just vacated. For a split second, he is tempted to go back, but a force compels him to lift his eyes towards the mountain. Adamos sucks in his breath, for the majestic mountain looks like a giant cone silhouetted against the moonlit sky.

"I can go up there and hide 'til morning," he whispers to himself. "If Eva can climb Fijora, so can I."

"You've never bothered before, why bother now?" says a voice. Adamos spins around. "Who said that? Who's there?"

"I'm your conscience, at least that's what you can call me for now. Answer my question: you've never been up there before, why now?"

"There's always a first time," argues Adamos.

"And what do you hope to find once you're up there?"

"Nothing … just looking for a place to pass the night." Adamos wishes the voice would shut up.

"And deal with your conscience?"

"Look, Eva says she finds solitude there. This I want to see."

"But you don't believe that to be true, Adamos."

"Hush up, will you?" Adamos' tone is harsh.

"And I suppose you think taking Eva's nuggets was the right thing to do."

"Of course, otherwise I wouldn't have done it. Look, who are you to speak to me this way?"

"I've already said. I'm your conscience, Adamos, something you should pay more attention to. If you're wise you won't go up there. You would return to your hut, replace Eva's nuggets, and be a loving, caring husband like you're supposed to."

"Get stuffed, conscience. I'm going up the mountain whether you approve or not. And one more thing, you have no right questioning my motives or telling me what I should and shouldn't do. I control you … you don't control me."

Adamos retraces his steps towards the base of the mountain. He begins his climb. Soon he comes to a fork. "Eh!" Adamos stops and stares at the two paths, confused as to which one he should take. A signpost helps him come to a decision: Scenic but rugged – 40 minutes. Gradual but winding – 1 hour, 45 minutes. "Why should I risk life and limb on a treacherous climb when I could breeze down the easy path?"

Adamos thinks he should lighten the load of his basket some more, before he continues his climb along the easy path. He spots a boulder beside the signpost. It is a good hiding place for his parcel of meat. He will retrieve it in the morning on his way down from the mountain.

Switching the makeshift sack of nuggets to the other shoulder, Adamos resumes his climb. It is not long before his legs begin to hurt and his heart hammers at the wall of his chest. His clothes are wet with sweat. He yanks the sack of nuggets off his shoulder and plops it into the basket. After a few exhalations, he resumes his climb. Under its unaccustomed load, the basket strains even more, and once again, Adamos slings one sack of nuggets across his shoulder.

Adamos feels he has been climbing for what seems like ages. He should have reached the summit by now. Perhaps he should have taken the rugged path. Pausing only to take a few deep breaths, Adamos presses on, determined to reach the summit.

Finally, soaked to the bone from sweating, Adamos reaches the summit. He wishes he had brought a change of clothing. Nevertheless, a broad smile creases his face. "Conscience, I did it," he says aloud with mock pride. "I made it to the top of this blasted mountain ... whoa ... this is one mother of a tree ..." His voice trails off as the gnarled branches of the old tree creek and groan softly in the breeze.

Suddenly, a light flickers, like a beacon warning ships of impending danger, at the entrance to the hollow at the center of the trunk. Adamos sucks in his breath, expecting to see someone holding a lamp. But no one comes out. He slides the leg of nuggets off his shoulder and dumps it into the basket.

"Must be my imagination," Adamos whispers, taking quick breaths to relax his racing heart. He is unable to resist the force, which draws him to the entrance of the gigantic tree. He almost stumbles over the stump, which serves as a seat inside the hollow trunk. Instinctively, he plants his large bottom upon it and props the heavy basket onto his lap. The quietness inside the tree does not escape him; goose bumps prickle his skin. He grips the basket tightly.

"What brings you here?" says an unfamiliar, yet familiar voice, startling Adamos.

"I ... I ... didn't realize there was someone here," Adamos stammers apologetically, looking around in the darkness. But there is no one. "Who's there?" he asks, mustering up enough courage to show he is not afraid.

"Just you and me, Adamos. I surround you."

"What? The tree? Don't be stupid, Adamos, trees can't talk," says

Adamos, thinking the tree has spoken. "It's only my flaming conscience playing up again."

"I'm much bigger than the tree ... the mountain even. I'm the Creator of all that is. I even reside in you. It will do you well to remember this."

"No, you listen, conscience," argues Adamos with brazen intent. "I am even bigger. I can control you. That should shut you up." Adamos bites down on his lower lip, but at the back of his mind, he is pondering why his conscience said it is the Creator of all that is. What exactly does that mean? And how is it possible his own conscience can make itself sound like another person speaking?

For a moment there is silence. Adamos relaxes, his fears assuaged. He opens and shuts his eyes, allowing them to adjust to the darkness. Things soon become more visible and he is able to focus on his surroundings. All he sees are giant, knobby roots and dead wood. He cannot understand why Eva and the other islanders waste their precious time trudging up the mountain just to sit in a hole in a tree looking at dead wood.

"They're just plain stupid, that's what," he says aloud, satisfied that it is, at least, a good place to rest. "If nothing else, it'll do for tonight. Tomorrow I'll be gone long before Eva gets here—if she gets here." Adamos bursts out laughing. "She won't get here," he muses. "Once she finds me gone and discovers that I've taken her precious nuggets, she will not have the energy or the will to come climbing up no mountain. I'll be safe as mud huts in a drought as long as I can hide from the others who come up here looking for a *piece of solitude*. Ah, how wonderful it feels to be free. How delectable it will be to acquire a new, obedient wife."

A wide grin stretches Adamos' chubby face as he wallows in his newfound freedom. He rocks the basket back and forth on his lap, before slipping it onto the ground beside his feet. "This sure is peaceful here," he says aloud, though he doesn't feel at ease.

"Isn't it, though?" The voice speaks again.

"Aye!" Adamos replies, glad now for any kind of conversation, if only with his conscience or even with the Creator—if that is what his conscience prefers to call itself.

"You've never bothered to come here before."

"Didn't see much point."

"And you do now?"

"Yep! But not for the reason you think."

"So why are you here, if it isn't for solitude?"

"Left home ... have nowhere to go just yet," confides Adamos.

"Left home? Why?"

"Eva, that's my irritating wife, is dull and boring ...."

"But a good provider, nonetheless."

"She doesn't really work, you know ... claims she has special talents, which she must use to help people. And get this: the fools actually believe her. They even give her food to show their appreciation. My wife has little brains ... and no logic ... always helping others when she should be helping me. I had to leave her, you see, to teach her a lesson."

"And what lesson is that, Adamos?"

"One that she isn't likely to forget once she finds me gone."

"And the lesson is?"

"That her place is to look after me, her husband."

"You mean slave for you, don't you?"

"Call it what you like. But I, Adamos, wear the pants, not her. I'm the husband, so I'm always right even when I know I'm wrong. This very night when Eva returns to the hut and finds me, and all her ... er ... my important possessions gone ... she will be crushed. She will live to regret the way she has treated ... er ... mistreated me."

"But did you have to take her nuggets as well?"

"Eh! How did you know that?" Adamos sucks in his breath, then smiles, thinking he is merely conversing with himself. "Sure. Wouldn't you? If she's stupid enough to think the nuggets strengthen her self-confidence, then I must prove different. If I strip her of the nuggets; I strip her of her so-called self-confidence. If I strip her of all she believes in, I strip her of her false sense of security. It's dead simple."

"How would you like to be stripped of all you have and are?"

"Now you sound as dumb as my wife. I can't be stripped of anything. Can't happen. I'm too smart to allow it," says Adamos. "Besides, all I have is in this basket. How can I be stripped when I have it all right here?"

"And you honestly believe stripping Eva of her nuggets will crush her spirit?"

"Just you watch." Adamos rubs his hands together.

"Then you're more of a fool than you think, Adamos. A man who finds a wife, finds a good thing."

He will ignore that. Bantering with his thoughts was harmless until those last comments, but he will not dignify those thoughts with a response. Instead, Adamos listens to his breathing, measuring the length of each exhalation. But the comments did bruise his ego. Against his better judgment, he lashes out. "It's you and my wife who are the bigger fools. Eva claims this place gives her solitude, and you claim to be the Creator." Adamos tightens his fists. "Now, that's a laugh. Solitude from a tree, and you the Creator? Ridiculous! Ha! Ha ha! Ha ha ha! I laugh with scorn at you and my pathetic wife. Pity I shan't be there to pick up the pieces when Eva breaks."

"Oh, you will, Adamos, you will ... only the joke will be on you."

Adamos bursts out laughing again. "This is stupid. Here I sit in the middle of an old tree trunk talking wildly to myself."

"And you really believe that, do you?"

"'Course I do. This conversation is all happening inside my head. I can block the thoughts anytime. Like not eating when I choose to."

"By the looks of you, you choose to eat all the time."

"Don't be so rude." Adamos' face muscles tightens.

"And you eat all the meat, leaving only vegetables— carrots and lettuce—for your hardworking wife. That's not nice, is it?"

"Look who's talking 'nice'! Where is she when I'm sick, eh? Tell me that." Adamos feels himself growing angry at the voice and draws a deep breath. He begins to clench and unclench his fists.

"Pretending you're sick you mean!"

Adamos is unable to respond to the truth. Perhaps he should stop arguing and the thoughts will go away. Adamos clamps his lips together, holds his breath for ten counts, before exhaling slowly through his nose. Amazingly, the thoughts stop, so too the nervous clenching of his fists. Adamos shifts his bottom on the stump to a more comfortable position. His eyes search the small enclosure for a place to lie down.

"How would you like to be stuck eating carrots and lettuce, Adamos?" The voice pierces the stillness like a thunderclap; Adamos topples off the stump.

Realizing his 'thoughts' are active again, Adamos picks himself up and resettles on the stump. He will simply refuse to answer.

"Well?" prompts the voice.

"Well what?" The words spill out before Adamos can stop them.

"How would you like to consume carrots and lettuce every day?"

"Never! That will never happen as long as Eva brings meat home. Anyway, I shan't be going back, ever. My quest now is to find me a new, obedient wife ... a proper wife who will cook proper meals. Now stifle yourself, conscience."

"Ah, Adamos, how luscious the grass appears on the other side!"

"Eh?" Adamos turns to stare out the entrance. For a split second he is fooled into thinking he can see a patch of green grass twinkling beyond the darkness. Instead, a flash of white light blinds him. The next moment he is sniffing the base of his basket. The intensity of the bright light must have caused him to fall off the stump, he surmises, making no effort to get up. The ground feels warm and comfortable and he is tired after the long hike up the mountain. His wet clothing has surprisingly dried completely. He curls into a ball. "I may as well lie here and sleep a while," he whispers, closing his eyes. "I'll worry about tomorrow when tomorrow comes." The smell of carrots emanating from the basket causes his nose to twitch. He feels a desire rising in his tummy, a queer craving for carrots and lettuce! "I'll have carrots for breakfast," he says with a yawn. "I'm too tired to bother chewing this late at night."

Soon Adamos is fast asleep and dreams about ... rabbits!

Five

It is late by the time Eva returns to the hut. She opens the door, wondering why Adamos has not bothered to keep the lamps burning. The inside of the hut feels different—hollow and empty. Eva lights a lamp.

"Adamos!" she whispers softly, looking at the outline on the grass-filled mattress. She smiles to herself; she is full with the stew Neena cooked for her. "Adamos!" she whispers again, creeping past the sleeping form. "Sorry I was so long and you couldn't wait up for me. Sleep well, my dear. I will not disturb you with counting the nuggets tonight. I'll just look at them, though, before I join you."

Taking the lamp over to the table, where the nuggets are stored, Eva settles the lamp onto the ground. She lifts her sewing basket off the table and places it beside the lamp. She shifts the tabletop to one side before tipping it off the base. Eva picks up the lamp and holds it over the hollow base. She sucks in her breath, almost dropping the lamp.

"Adamos!" Eva shouts, her eyes wide with disbelief. "We have been robbed. Adamos, wake up. Come and see. All my nuggets are gone except ... oh, Adamos." She reaches into the box and gathers the few nuggets that remain. "Ten!" She lets the nuggets sift through her fingers. "Will you not wake, Adamos? Someone has robbed us."

Eva slumps her shoulders and shakes her head. She feels sick. Who could have done such a horrible thing? No one on the island has ever committed any crimes. She looks at the motionless form on the mattress and crosses over to it.

"Wake up, Adamos." Eva bends over to give the bulky lump a gentle shake, but her hand grasps only cloth. "Hah!" she says, springing back. With the toe of her boot, she prods the softness, then reaches down and peels the covers away.

"What!" Eva staggers backwards as realization dawns. Adamos

is gone—so too is the parcel of boar meat. "It is Adamos who has absconded with my nuggets." Eva covers her face with her hands. "Why, Adamos, why have you done this deed? Have I not been a good wife to you all these years in spite of your constant insults? Have you gone back to … her? No! I must not think that thought." Eva inhales deeply, then blows the breath out noisily through her mouth. She must think rationally.

"Perhaps the nuggets were not mine to keep in the first place," she tells herself. "Then again, perhaps Adamos is only trying to make me worry and will return in the night, when he is sure I'm asleep."

Eva decides to make her bed far away from the one she shares with Adamos. It will comfort her if she pretends all is well in the hut and Adamos is asleep in the far corner. Her belly is full; she will sleep well.

Eva nestles under her covers, but sleep escapes her. She thinks about the conversation she has had with her sister that evening.

"Sister, dear, I don't know why you keep Adamos. He's lazy and useless. What does he do for you? He treats you worse than a flea, yet you are devoted to him. Me, your only sister, he despises. I can't come near your hut without him barking insults at me. What does he think, Eva? Does he think I have the black plague or something? And what about your friends, Eva? You have none … because of him and his silly behavior."

"When you have a husband you will understand," she had said.

"You must be joking, Eva. I want no husband if he will be anything like Adamos."

"Neena, don't carry on so," she had replied gently. "Perhaps Adamos is unaware of his bad behavior. Perhaps it is my fault for not teaching him the ways of a proper husband. Tonight I will talk to him."

"Too late for that, Eva. He will not listen. Never has. The only thing that talks to Adamos is food. One day, he will walk away when he thinks he no longer needs you to feed him."

Eva sucks in her breath. The truth of her sister's words jolts her back to the present. Aloud she says, "No, Neena, you are wrong. Adamos will not do such a thing. He will be back this night." Even so,

Eva still cannot understand why Adamos needed to take her nuggets.

It is past midnight by the time Eva drifts off to sleep, only to wake some time later to whisperings in her ear.

"Eva! Make haste. Go to the mountain."

Eva springs up. "Adamos, you've come back. I knew you would … Adamos, dear Adamos?"

There is no one else in the little hut; Adamos' bed is still empty. She realizes it is the Great Pine speaking, which stirred her from sleep. It is at least an hour earlier than she is used to getting up. But she must do as she has been instructed and make haste to the mountain. Perhaps the Great Pine has news about Adamos.

Moonlight guides her footsteps up the rugged path to the summit of the mountain. Her progress is slow because she ponders how and what she will say to the tree.

Meanwhile, in the stillness of the hollow of the Great Pine, Adamos stirs. A voice whispers in his ear, "Rise, Adamos. Rise and eat."

"What? Now?" groans Adamos, rolling onto his side. He feels warm, as if someone has wrapped him in a furry blanket.

"Yes, now," says the voice.

Remembering where he is, Adamos sniffs. The smell of raw carrots pierces his nostrils. Suddenly, he thinks carrots are exactly what he wants to eat. Adamos stretches out his hand to grab one. "Oh!" he shrieks, pulling back. The hand that reached for the carrot is not his. *The moonlight must be playing tricks,* he thinks. "Don't be such a fool, Adamos," he chides, reaching out again to grasp the carrot. Again it is not his hand he sees—but a small furry paw, yet he seems able to control it.

"Who has done this dreadful thing to me?" cries Adamos, staring at the white furry paw. Adamos moves the paw away from the carrot and rubs it against his cheek. Another shock awaits him. He has grown whiskers! He feels his ears and finds they have grown longer. "This is madness," says Adamos, his heart pounding. "This must be a bad dream. It isn't possible. It cannot be. How can I have changed into a rabbit? I hate rabbits." Remembering the nuggets, Adamos looks for the basket only to discover he is blocked in all directions by bars and there is no sign of the basket or the nuggets.

"Oh, no," he breathes, "I'm trapped in a cage! Eva's nuggets are gone! How did I get into the cage? What am I to do now?" Adamos gnaws at the bars, before sinking his sharp teeth into a carrot.

"Having trouble, Adamos?"

"That's an understatement," replies Adamos. "Let me guess. It had to be you who turned me into a bloody rabbit, stuck me in this cage, and now you ask if I'm having trouble? You call yourself wise?"

"More wise than you think, Adamos."

"But why am I in a cage?"

"To keep you safe, Adamos, during transportation."

"Transportation? Where to?"

"To your new home."

"My new home?"

"Stop repeating everything I say, Adamos. I happen to know your hearing is acute."

"What have you done with the nuggets? Tell me," Adamos demands.

"They're safe. That's all you need to know."

"The joke's over. Turn me back into a man and return the nuggets."

"Why?"

"So I can ... er ... return to my wife."

"But you left her and took her nuggets, Adamos."

"It was only for a joke ... to prove a point."

"Then you should have listened to your conscience and returned to the hut when you had the chance."

"Everyone makes mistakes," argues Adamos.

"And they must ultimately face the consequences."

"So I'm to remain in this altered state, then?"

"That's up to you."

"You changed me into a rabbit, and it's up to me if I'm to remain a rabbit or not? You don't make any sense. How am I supposed to make myself a man again, eh Mr. Creator? Am I supposed to say 'abracadabra-jiggety-jig monkey's-whalebone-nuts and fried bananas? Tell me!"

"Figure it out for yourself, Adamos. Figure it out."

The discussion over, Adamos resigns himself to sleep.

Six

The early morning breeze is slightly cool as Eva climbs the mountain. She stops only to inhale deep breaths of dew-moistened air. She looks up towards the summit. It seems different in the moonlight, as if burdened.

"Perhaps the Great Pine knows about the nuggets," says Eva, resuming her trek up the mountain. The rustle of branches and leaves, swaying softly with every breath of wind, adds melody to Eva's rhythmic heartbeat. She lifts her face to the wind and smiles, surprised to find her heart is no longer troubled at the loss of the nuggets or Adamos' disappearance.

By the time Eva reaches the summit, her legs are tired and she pauses for a moment to regain some strength. When refreshed, she steps through the entrance to the hollow of the Great Pine. She plants her bottom on the stump, clasping her hands together and pulling her shoulders back. She does not speak, but waits for the gentle voice and comforting touch she has come to cherish. Neither come.

It seems like forever that Eva sits in silence. "Perhaps it is I who should first speak," she whispers, rolling her thumbs over each other. She clears her throat. "Great Pine," she begins, her voice soft and controlled, "I was awakened earlier than usual and told to come up here." Eva pauses, waiting for a response, but receives none.

"Is it because I've ... er ... lost the nuggets? I ... I ... am sorry, but ...," she continues in a broken whisper.

"Did you say 'lost the nuggets,' Eva?" says the voice at last.

"Yes, I mean ..." Eva is bewildered.

"No, Eva, you haven't lost the nuggets. They were taken, and do you know who took them?"

Eva is too embarrassed to admit her own husband has stolen her precious nuggets. She bows her head.

"Eva," prompts the voice, "will you tell me who took the nuggets?"

There is no point lying, thinks Eva. *I must tell what I believe to be the truth.* "Great Pine," she says, pausing for a breath, "forgive me if I am wrong, for it is not right to accuse anyone without proof, but Adamos is gone and so are all but ten of the nuggets. It is he who took the nuggets."

"Yes, Eva! Gone indeed is Adamos with the nuggets. I will not chastise you for neglecting to keep the nuggets in a safer place. What Adamos has done is pitiful."

"Will you forgive him for the thoughtless deed he has committed?"

"Forgive Adamos?" says the voice, calmly. "After what he has done, you ask for his forgiveness?"

"Yes. I will get over the pain of losing Adamos, but will he survive his conscience, for it will haunt him?"

"I will consider your request, Eva. But this I want you to do. Beside your left foot is a cage. Inside the cage is a rabbit. I want you to care for the animal."

"A rabbit?" whispers Eva, looking down beside her left foot. Her eyes widen. From the moonlight seeping into the hollow, the cage glitters with a yellow light. Inside the cage, she sees a white rabbit with a pink bow around its neck. The rabbit is fast asleep. Eva picks up the cage and, holding it at arms length, stares at the rabbit. Remembering her childhood vow about never wanting another rabbit to replace her beloved Hoppippa, Eva says, "Couldn't I have a bird instead?"

"Perhaps another time, Eva ... but this rabbit needs your help ... and a home."

"It is so fat," she says. "What help can I give a fat rabbit?"

"Make it thin again, Eva," says the voice.

Eva does not answer. The cage weighs heavily on her extended arm and she places it on her lap. She stares at the rabbit more closely. Suddenly, its eyes pop open and their eyes lock. The rabbit springs up, instantly thumping its head on the roof of the cage.

"Eva!" twitches the whiskers. "You are here already? I was not ... I should have been gone before you came."

Eva's heart skips a beat. Something about the rabbit's eyes alarms her. They are blue-green like Adamos'. "Great Pine," she says, "I cannot take this rabbit."

"And why not, Eva?" The voice is gentle.

"It's on account of the eyes. They remind me of Adamos'. Let me not have this added burden. I want only to forget him now."

"That may be so, Eva. I can do nothing about the eyes, but the rabbit needs a home and I remember how you came to me once before when your own pet rabbit died. You wanted me to make it live again, only it wasn't possible. Now, I'm asking you to care for this one, shall we say, in exchange for losing the nuggets. When it becomes thin again, you can certainly return it if, by then, you don't want to keep it. Fair?"

Eva studies the restless rabbit.

"Eva," says Adamos, hoping she might realize he is the rabbit, "it is I, Adamos, who is in the cage. Do not agree to take me away, my love, for I must remain here if I'm to become a man ... your loving husband ... again."

Eva does not hear. All she sees is a frantic twitching of mouth and whiskers. *A rabbit is a rabbit,* she thinks. *What harm can it do? I don't have to look at its eyes.* "Very well," says Eva. "I will make it thin. A diet of carrots and lettuce should do the trick."

"Indeed it would. So you agree to take the animal?"

"Yes." Eva shuffles her feet. "Does it have a name, then?"

"You can give it any name you like, Eva. Suit yourself."

Eva stands, lifting the cage as she does so. "I will go now, Great Pine. Thank you for the rabbit."

"And take good care of the cage, too."

"I will."

Sunlight is already peeping through the clouds, warming the air. Eva descends the mountain, following the rugged path as usual. Adamos is surprised at this, but is overwhelmed when he sees the amazing vista. The cage swings and bounces, and he struggles to maintain his balance.

"Flaming Nora! Please, Eva, don't bounce the cage so. It makes me nauseous. Perhaps it's because I'm not used to this new body."

Eva pays no attention to the troubled rabbit. She hums softly, her thoughts focused on planting cassava roots, her feet travel down the familiar path with ease.

"I shouldn't have been so greedy, Eva," says Adamos, twitching his unaccustomed whiskers. He spreads his hind legs to steady himself and grasps the side of the cage with his front paws, in a feeble attempt to ease the effects of his turbulent ride. "Already I ... I regret being so selfish in my attitude toward you. I shouldn't have been so arrogant toward the tree either. Now look at me ... trapped in a cage ... in the body of a rabbit for crying out loud!"

Another bounce sends Adamos tumbling head over heels. Sprawled on his tummy, he grasps the lower bars of the cage with his paws. Suddenly he spies the boulder behind which he has hidden the parcel of boar meat.

"Stop, Eva. I must retrieve the meat. It will spoil ... or worse, be devoured by flipping rodents."

But Eva strides past the boulder. Bones crunch in Adamos' neck when he turns his head to stare grudgingly at the retreating boulder harboring his precious meat. "Stop!" One paw stretches towards the boulder.

"Oh, what's the use." Adamos sniffs, retracting his paw. "Eva cannot hear or understand me. What is to become of me? Oh how I wish I could turn back the hands of time. I would never have climbed this blasted mountain."

Adamos' heart is full of remorse, not because of the meat, or even the lost nuggets, but mainly because of the unfortunate predicament in which he finds himself.

Seven

At last, Eva reaches the base of the mountain. A few more hurried steps and she stands in front of the door to her hut. Although a full day's work is ahead of her, she knows she must first leave the rabbit inside the hut. Forgetting Adamos is not there, she bursts into the little room.

"Adamos, look …!" But the quietness soon reminds her of his absence. She clamps her lips together, finishing the sentence in her mind: *The Great Pine has given me a rabbit.*

Eva plonks the cage onto the table, but avoids looking at the animal, for she does not want to look into its eyes. "I will not feed you yet, fat rabbit." Eva stares at the wall behind the rabbit as she speaks, avoiding any chance of accidental eye contact. "Truth is, rabbit, I don't like you at all because your eyes remind me of my thieving, selfish husband. And he was just as fat as you. If you ask me, I'd say it is him who needs slimming more than you."

"Eva," interrupts Adamos, twitching his whiskers, "you do not miss me? You do not care that you are alone?" Adamos is heartbroken.

But Eva cannot hear him. "Tell me, rabbit, do you steal?" For the first time she allows her anger to possess her. "Will you eat all my meat if I let you run free in the hut when I'm out? Adamos used to do that. He used to stuff all day long. Only he didn't think I knew; he always said the meat turned bad and he had to throw it out. No wonder he kept getting like a balloon."

Eva glances briefly at the rabbit. The sight of it moping in the corner of the cage with its eyes shut calms her. "Of course you can't answer, can you, rabbit? Sorry I lost my temper. You're not to blame for the way I feel. Maybe I'll leave you in the cage for today so you can get used to your new surroundings. Tonight, when I return from work, I'll let you out. I might even feed you then."

As Eva turns to leave, Adamos springs forward. "Please, Eva, don't leave me like this. I'm here. I'm the rabbit. Look into my eyes, my love. I know you hate me for running off with your nuggets, but believe me, I'm truly sorry. It was the stupidest thing to do. Already I can see I've made a big mistake ... and I'm sorry about the food too."

Adamos reaches above his head, and grabbing the side of the cage with his front paws, pulls himself up. His back legs tremble, struggling to support the weight of his body.

"Eva, my absence doesn't perturb you?" His twitching whiskers poke through the gaps between the bars. "I know now it is I who must change, not you. Please, you must help me become my former self so that I can right the wrongs I've done to you. Please take me back to the tree, I beg you."

Adamos realizes his pleas are useless because Eva is unable to understand the squeaking of a rabbit. After Eva leaves for work, Adamos does what he does best—he resigns himself to sleep. But his raging, tormented thoughts do not allow him a restful sleep.

Outside the hut, Eva fills her lungs with the freshness of the morning air. With Adamos gone, so too is the burden of his morning insults. She will carry on as she always has and let her chores fill the emptiness in her heart. Any more thoughts of the rabbit in her care are quickly replaced with the needs of the people she has promised to help that day. First, she will visit her sister to see if the fenced enclosure is large enough for the wild pigs or if it needs to be expanded. Once that is done, she will then check with farmer Ohuna to see if he needs to plant any more carrots or cassava roots. Last of all, she will call on Tulisa and Bragga, who are to be married in two weeks, to see if they have chosen a site for their new hut.

"Yes," whispers Eva, taking a long, appreciative look at the mountain, "I've a busy day ahead. Adamos, wherever you might be, find happiness." Eva adjusts the bag on her shoulder. "Tonight I will blindfold the rabbit." She whistles softly as she charges towards her sister's hut.

Neena is already feeding the wild pigs when Eva arrives.

"Good morning, sister dear," Eva sings out, her voice light.

"Eva! Morning!" Neena smiles welcomingly, for she is always thrilled to see her older sister. "You sound cheerful. How is that lazy, fat husband of yours this morn?"

Eva is slow replying. Only last night her sister had said Adamos would run off one day. Should she admit now that she was right, or should she cover up? Eva has never lied to her sister, but to talk negatively to anyone about Adamos will cause her throat to hurt.

"Eva? You hesitate. Why?"

Eva clears her throat softly and lifts her eyes to meet her sister's. "You were right."

"Right? About what, sister dear?"

"About Adamos."

"That he's fat and lazy?"

"And the rest."

"The rest?" Neena narrows her eyes, regarding her sister with intent curiosity. "You mean he has left you?" One thought hammers in Neena's head: *After all these years, Adamos has gone back to her.* Yes, she knows Eva's secret, but has said nothing to Eva, because she wasn't sure if Eva knew. She will continue to pretend ignorance of the matter, for Eva's sake. "Well? Has he?"

Slowly Eva nods.

Neena bursts out laughing. "Then you should be happy. The louse. You deserve better. Besides, at forty-five, Adamos is an old man. Look for a younger man, Eva."

"And there's more," says Eva, unable to quell the unexpected emotions that cause words to spew out of her mouth. This was worth a sore throat!

"More? What more can there be, Eva?" Neena's laughter disappears and a worried look creases her forehead. "Has he destroyed your hut? Tell me." Neena's hands curl into tight fists at her sides.

"No, Neena, nothing like that." Eva considers whether this is the right time to tell her sister about the nuggets. Will she believe her?

Then, remembering she still has the last nugget in her pocket, she decides the moment has come to reveal all to her beloved sister ... but still she hesitates.

"Let me help you finish feeding the pigs," says Eva, "and I will help with whatever chores you have left, then over a steaming cup of berry tea and some pancakes, I'll tell you everything."

Neena reaches out and rubs her sister's shoulder affectionately. "Very well, sister, but you must promise not to leave anything out. If Adamos has hurt you in any way, I want to know."

"And you will," replies Eva, dropping her shoulder bag on the ground and reaching for a bucket of slop.

Together the two sisters make short order of Neena's morning chores. Eva mends the fence of the wild pigs' enclosure. She is surprised how happy she feels inside, in spite of the loss of her nuggets and the disappearance of Adamos. The image of the fat rabbit, restrained in its cage, floods into her mind, and she smiles. "I must blindfold those pitiful eyes which are so much like Adamos'," she whispers.

Finishing their chores, the sisters wash their hands at the nearby stream, before settling in Neena's cozy hut for tea and pancakes.

"Now, tell me," encourages Neena, taking a sip of berry tea.

"Where do I begin?" says Eva, more to herself.

"At the beginning is always best," replies Neena. "I have time to listen. How much time do you have before your next job?" Neena knows Eva enjoys offering her services to whoever needs them, and asks nothing in return. She could never explain, though, how Eva acquired her extraordinary abilities and she has never asked. Always she knew if Eva wanted to tell her, she would.

After a second bite of her pancake, which she washes down with a mouthful of tea, Eva leans her elbows on the table and begins her story. She finds it easy to recount the time when she was eight and had climbed the mountain to tell the Great Pine about the death of her beloved rabbit. She tells Neena about the extraordinary gifts and the knowledge, patience, and compassion she had acquired once she came down from the mountain. She tells Neena that, every evening, when she returns home, she always finds a small yellow nugget under the mat at the front door of her hut. She tells Neena about Adamos eating all the food during the day and then lying about why there is none left for her. She tells Neena about the painful insults Adamos showers on her each morning before she leaves for the mountain.

"All this you kept to yourself, Eva?" Neena interrupts, feeling her own anger rising, amazed at her sister's inner strength.

Eva smiles. "The Great Pine gives me the strength to cope, Neena. But, there is more." Eva pauses. She shifts her bottom on the tree stump used for a seat, assuming a more comfortable position. She struggles to restrain the thoughts of what she would like to do to Adamos when she gets hold of him. Neena's voice, urging her to continue, snaps her back to the present.

"Last night," says Eva, "before I brought you the boar's meat to cook, I told Adamos when I returned we would count the nuggets. By the way he reacted, I should have guessed he didn't want me anywhere near the nuggets."

"What do you mean, Eva?"

"He said, according to legend, it wasn't good to count nuggets at night."

"Legend? What legend? I know of no such thing, Eva."

"Aye! Neither do I. And neither does Adamos, I'm sure."

"So, did you count these … nuggets?"

Eva breaks into laughter. "No! You see, when I returned home after your lovely meal, Adamos was fast asleep, or so I thought. As I didn't want to disturb him with the noise of jingling nuggets, I decided just to look at them. I shifted the top off the table as quietly as I could … that's where I store the nuggets … in the box which forms the base of the table. When I held the lamp light above the box … I only saw ten nuggets." Eva pauses and draws in a deep breath.

"Ten! But you said you had been gathering them for years." Neena leans forward, her eyes wide with disbelief.

Eva nods. "So I have, and by my reckoning, I should have hundreds of them."

"What are these nuggets? What do they look like?"

Eva reaches into her pocket and extracts one of the nuggets. "Here. They do nothing, except build my self-confidence ... a reward for all I do, I guess."

Neena takes the nugget. "'Tis small ... but heavy, Eva. I've never seen anything like it. You must be truly blessed to be given such an unusual reward, dear sister." Neena is awestruck.

"Indeed. Anyway, let me continue. I called out to Adamos that we had been robbed, but his great lump remained shiftless under the blankets. When I tried to rouse him from sleep, I was shocked to discover the mound under the blankets wasn't Adamos ... just a pile of old clothes and blankets. He had absconded with the lot, leaving only ten nuggets."

"The lousy rat!"

"'Perhaps it was not meant for me to keep the nuggets,' I said to myself. 'Perhaps Adamos just wants to make me worry ... and he will return in the night.' I made my bed away from Adamos' and pretended he was still there, asleep. Early this morning, long before dawn, a voice awakened me, commanding me to go to the mountain. I thought Adamos had returned ... only he hadn't. So I went to the mountain, wondering how I would explain the loss of the nuggets to the Great Pine." Eva pauses.

"So, what happened?"

"Well, the Great Pine asked if I knew who had stolen the nuggets. I was embarrassed to admit it was Adamos, but I couldn't lie to the Great Pine, so I confessed. Then, to my surprise, the Great Pine said, 'Yes, you are right, Eva. Gone indeed has Adamos, but I will not chastise you for not keeping the nuggets in a safer place. But this I want you to do. Beside your left foot is a cage. Inside the cage is a rabbit. I want you to care for the animal.' I was astonished at this, of course. I do not want another rabbit, and a fat one at that. So I refused, but the Great Pine wouldn't hear of it. Said I should make the rabbit thin again, only then could I return it. It was no use arguing. So I agreed, but I cannot look at the rabbit's eyes, Neena."

"Why not? What's wrong with the eyes, Eva?"

"They remind me of Adamos."

Neena bursts out laughing.

"You think that's funny, Neena?"

"A crazy picture ... just flashed ... through my mind," says Neena in between shafts of laughter and inhalations. "Maybe the fat rabbit is really Adamos."

"Don't be stupid, dear. How can a man change into a rabbit? That's preposterous." But she, too, bursts out laughing, allowing herself to see the funny side of what her sister has said.

The sisters laugh so much, tears pour down their cheeks. Finally spent, Eva is the first to gather her thoughts. "Would serve him right if he did become a rabbit," she says, blowing her nose into an old handkerchief. "Bit by bit Adamos chips away at me, hoping to break my spirit, hoping in the end, he will be all I have, and need." Eva pauses but only for a second. "But as much as we would like the rabbit to be Adamos, it isn't possible, and I am left with the chore of slimming it ... I'm already looking forward to returning the stupid thing."

"So how will you do it, Eva? Slim the animal, I mean."

"I suppose I will have to cut down on its intake—perhaps feed it two small pieces of carrots and half a leaf of lettuce every other day, for the first two weeks. That should be a good start, don't you think, Neena?"

"You're supposed to make the animal thin, not starve it to death." Neena breaks into peals of laughter again.

"Aye! If I knew for sure the rabbit was Adamos, I might be tempted to do just that. Starve it to death."

"I can't help my instincts." Neena's voice takes on a more serious tone; there is no shaking the thought within her head.

"Instincts? What instincts?"

"About the rabbit being a possible reincarnation of Adamos."

Eva rolls her eyes upwards. "I don't believe Adamos is dead, Neena. Don't say such things."

"He might as well be."

Suddenly Eva wants to talk no more about Adamos or the rabbit. She jumps up. "I must go now, Neena. I promised to help farmer

Ohuna plant cassava roots."

"Have your meal with me tonight, Eva. Stay the night, perhaps," Neena insists.

"And what about the rabbit? Another time, eh?" Eva clears her throat. It feels dry, but not sore.

"It's safe and warm. It will not miss you."

"Maybe not, but it has to be fed at least something tonight."

Eva leaves then, and hurries off to help farmer Ohuna, who is already in the field planting cassava roots.

Eight

It is still light by the time Eva returns home with an ample supply of farmer Ohuna's scrumptious muttonbird stew and a few carrots. At the front door, she lifts the mat and finds ten yellow nuggets.

"Adamos has returned!" exclaims Eva, a surge of joy rushing through her body. But the joy soon dies. "No, it cannot be. He doesn't know this is where I find the nuggets."

Disappointed, Eva gathers the nuggets. "This time Adamos will not get his sticky paws on them … if he returns," whispers Eva. "I will hide them in a different place." She kicks the door open. She must avoid looking at the rabbit's eyes. Cautiously, she lifts her eyes to find the rabbit is fast asleep.

"Just like Adamos," says Eva. "I wouldn't be surprised if it slept all day. Maybe now is a good time to put the blindfold on."

Eva tiptoes past the rabbit and hurries into the kitchen, leaving a delicious aroma of the cooked stew in her wake. The rabbit stirs. Its whiskers twitch. Its pink tongue darts out, licking its lips in hungry anticipation.

"Ah," says Adamos, stretching lazily. "Eva has returned and has brought muttonbird stew. It's a long time since I had muttonbird. EVA! FEED ME. I'M STARVING. BRING ME SOME MUTTONBIRD … WITH LOTS OF CARROTS! Perhaps I shouldn't shout so. I must try some gentleness. Eva my sweet, I'm hungry, feed me."

Adamos sniffs the air expectantly, savoring the smell of the stew. When Eva does not return, he pushes his rabbit mouth between two bars, and says, "Eva my sweet, perhaps you didn't hear me; food, please!"

In the kitchen, Eva plops her bag on the ground and puts the food on the table. She drops the nuggets in a cup and hides it behind several jars of assorted herb and tea leaves which are stacked on one corner of the ground.

From a bundle of old clothes, Eva pulls out her worn-out pantaloons. "This is perfect for a blindfold," she says, removing the strings from the waist and legs. "The rabbit didn't have to have eyes like Adamos', did it?" Eva mumbles ripping a strip from the fabric.

Returning from the kitchen with the strip of cloth, Eva finds the rabbit sniffing the air. She braces herself for a face-to-face encounter. She will have to endure one last look at its eyes. Inhaling deeply, she walks to the cage. The rabbit crouches on its four paws, its whiskers twitching, its eyes looking steadily at Eva. It makes soft purring sounds like a cat. Eva purses her lips and, reaching into the cage, grabs the animal. It feels wet!

"Ah! Eva, you're taking me out of this wet prison at last. You know it's me, don't you? You're going to feed me, aren't you? Oh my darling wife, how I've misjudged your kindness. How I've missed your gentleness. I have memories of once upon a time when I whispered sweet words of nothingness into your ear, and held you lovingly in my arms. Let me rest my cheek against your bosom." Adamos almost chokes over these unaccustomed terms of endearment. All the same, he is overjoyed because he is free from his confinement in the cage. But his happiness evaporates when Eva quickly wraps a strip of cloth round and round his head, covering his eyes.

"NOOOOooooo!" screams Adamos, heaving his bulky rabbit body and twisting his head, trying to wriggle free from the blindfold. "You must not do this thing, Eva, my precious love. My eyes are the only means I have to convey to you that I am your *beloved* husband." The words almost stick in his throat. "Eva, noooooo!"

But Adamos' screams are in vain because Eva cannot hear him. Thinking the rabbit is trying to escape, Eva tightens her legs, clamping the short chunky paws between her knees; the wriggling stops.

What's the use? thinks Adamos. *I'm doomed.*

After wrapping the strip of cloth around the rabbit's eyes, without trapping its ears, Eva is satisfied she can now look at the animal without fear of it reminding her of Adamos.

"Now, there's a good rabbit," coos Eva, stroking the top of its head. "I shall have to place some absorbing padding at the bottom of your cage so when you pee it doesn't wet your fur."

"Yeah! Yeah!" Adamos jerks his head away, annoyed at Eva's callousness. "Like you really care! All the same, where do I do the other thing? I can't use the cesspit now, can I? I might fall in. Not that you would give a toss if I did ... fall in ... and die ... a slow ... painful ... drowning death."

Eva begins to sing softly.

The rabbit's whiskers twitch. "Stop singing, will you? Your voice irritates me ... you know that." Adamos is in a fowl mood now.

"A blindfolded rabbit with twitching whiskers; you look funny," says Eva with a laugh.

"Well, at least it's stopped you singing. So where do I do the other thing, darn it? I have a good mind to do it in your lap. Pity I don't have the urge just yet."

Grabbing an old rag, Eva rubs the rabbit dry. Still holding the animal, she folds some of Adamos' old clothing and lines the bottom of the cage.

"There you are, rabbit, a nice dry bed to sleep on. Pee on it as much as you like. Adamos won't be needing his shirts anymore."

"No, Eva, don't put me back in the cage." The rabbit's front paws lash out and wrap around Eva's arm. "Let me sleep on my bed ... our bed."

"You're a feisty little thing, aren't you?" Disengaging the paws, Eva plops the animal back into its cage.

Immediately the rabbit rolls onto its side—gasping for breath, wriggling feebly.

"With all that fat, I don't expect you're hungry." Eva prods the bulging tummy. "But I suppose I shouldn't be too harsh just yet. The shock of starving you might be too drastic, plus I don't want to find a dead rabbit in this lovely cage. Mind you, if you were Adamos, I would probably starve you, or accidentally drop you in the cesspit."

Yeah! I'm sure you would, thinks Adamos.

For the first time, Eva is able to look closely at the rabbit's cage. She is shocked to discover it is no ordinary cage. It is made of the same material as her nuggets, and the pattern is intricately woven. Her eyes widen. Leaning close to the side of the cage, she pokes her finger in and scratches the rabbit's ear. "What kind of rabbit are you to be given such a beautiful cage?" she whispers.

"I'm your husband, darn it. Your husband!" replies Adamos with rising anger, then in a resigned voice, he says, "Oh, what's the use?"

"Pity you can't talk, rabbit, otherwise you would probably tell me you are from a royal rabbit family," Eva teases. "I've news for you though; there are no royal rabbits or royal rabbit robes; no royal rabbit bedchambers or royal rabbit coaches. So I will not address you as Your Royal Rabbitness. You might have been somebody's pet, but you're a rabbit nonetheless." Eva tickles the rabbit's chin, humming softly to it.

Adamos twitches his whiskers, irritation mixed with remorse nips at his heartstrings. "Thanks for the reminder, Eva. A rabbit I am, a rabbit I will remain. That's my reward for the greed and pain I have caused you. I have no one to blame but myself. Oh, if I could turn back the hands of time, I would be a different person. I would be loving and kind towards you, the one true love of my life. I have seen the gentleness and love in you, Eva, only I chose to ignore it. Already I've seen the error of my ways."

"You twitch your whiskers as if you try to speak," says Eva. "Pity you can neither understand nor speak. It would be interesting to know what you think of that louse Adamos."

"Oh Eva, my sweet, I hear you. It is you who cannot hear me," twitches the whiskers. "You ask what I think of Adamos? You are right. He is a louse. I have seen how people are charmed by your smile and elegant ways. I have seen the way you lovingly do your chores, never complaining. But alas, this feeling of jealousy inside me was too strong to control and I ended up treating you miserably, my darling wife, always looking for ways to belittle you in front of others; never saying "please" or "thanks" when I asked you to do things for me. Why keep a dog if I have to bark myself, I always said to you. I am not a man; I am a lousy mouse. No, no, no, I am not a mouse at all. I am a flaming, lousy rabbit, but nonetheless, your husband."

The rabbit sighs; Eva withdraws her finger.

"That sigh," whispers Eva, staring at the rabbit. "It sounded like Adamos'. No!" She shakes her head to dislodge the emerging picture. Her sister's words flood back to her mind. *Maybe the fat rabbit is Adamos!* "No!" Eva backs away from the cage. "My mind is playing stupid tricks. You cannot be Adamos, rabbit. He is almost bald. If you were Adamos, you would have little hair on your head too." She laughs nervously. Her argument is logical, not illogical.

The rabbit presses its body against the side of the cage. "Eva," the whiskers vibrate, "you heard right. Yes, it is I, Adamos. I am the rabbit. That confounded tree has done this deed. Take me to it."

Ignoring the rabbit, Eva hurries back to the kitchen. She must dismiss those foolish thoughts. Eva braces her hands on the table. She must stop imagining such ridiculous things or she might go out of her mind. It is Neena's fault for planting the thought in her head in the first place. Adamos is gone and that is the end of that. From now on, she will focus on her promise.

"The faster I slim the thing, the faster I can return it to the tree." She decides to get the rabbit a small feeding of carrots and lettuce leaves, and a bowl of water.

After preparing the food, Eva returns to the cage. "Brought your meal, rabbit … carrots and lettuce," she says with sharpness, slipping the food through the door of the cage. But the rabbit remains dormant. "Are you not hungry?"

"I will not eat unless you remove this stupid blindfold, Eva," says Adamos, turning his rabbit head aside; pawing at his blindfold.

"Oh, I get it. You're annoyed because you cannot see to eat. Well, no worries, I will help." Eva picks up a piece of carrot and rubs it on the rabbit's lips, but the rabbit makes no effort to open its mouth.

"Suit yourself," says Eva, "starve if you prefer, I don't care, but I am hungry. While you decide whether you wish to eat or not, I will get myself some muttonbird stew."

Eva hurries into the kitchen and soon returns with a bowl of stew. She sits beside the rabbit's cage. The aroma of the muttonbird stew and vegetables wafts into the cage. The rabbit twitches its nose; the smell of the meat in the stew stirs its appetite. *Perhaps I have been too hasty in deciding not to eat while the blindfold is still on,* thinks Adamos.

"How about some muttonbird, then?" squeaks Adamos, thumping his hind paw on a lettuce leaf. "I don't like raw carrots and lettuce. Give me some stew. Oh, what's the use, Eva, you cannot hear me. If it weren't for this stupid blindfold, I could convince you I am your Adamos. Oh, what's the use, eh?"

Eva spoons several loads of the meaty stew into her mouth before catching a glimpse of the rabbit's rapidly twitching nose and thumping back paw. "Smells good, this stew, doesn't it, rabbit?" she says. "At last I can enjoy some meat in my food. Adamos used to eat all of it before I came home. 'The meat went bad, Eva, I had to throw it out.' My foot he had to throw it out! The lazy pig filled his belly all day and I had to eat carrots and lettuce for my dinner. Imagine he had the nerve to tell me how much trouble he went to, preparing the vegetables."

With every harsh expression and reminder of his deplorable behavior, Adamos cringes as if Eva has been striking him with a stick.

"Why do you jerk so, rabbit? Do you dislike my story? Or is it that you think what I think—that Adamos is a horrible pig?" Eva laughs. "How silly I sound, talking to an animal."

"You have every right to speak harsh words, Eva, they bring me to my senses. I'm sorry for being such a donkey. I feel regret for what I've done."

"Adamos used to go out to the cliffs looking for muttonbirds and the eggs they each laid in season. 'The taste of the meat is like no other,' he would say, 'and the egg a delicacy, my love,'" Eva explains to the rabbit, waving her wooden spoon in the air. One droplet of stew flies from the spoon and lands on the tip of the rabbit's nose. "But that was a long time ago, when we were first married." She sighs.

"Don't remind me," twitches the whiskers. Adamos stretches his tongue to lick the precious stew off his nose.

"There was even a time when he went deep-sea fishing for marlin with some of the men," says Eva. "But that, too, was a long time ago. Now he waits greedily for me to bring meat home. The lazy beggar ... he leaves me to do all the work, while he stuffs himself with food."

"I said don't remind me. Just let me have some flipping muttonbird," Adamos pleads; the tip of his pink tongue darts in and out of his mouth, licking spittle dripping down the side of his mouth.

Eva finishes her stew, except for one piece of meat. Just as she stands to take her bowl to the kitchen, someone bangs on the front door.

"Eva, it's me, Neena."

"Neena!" say Adamos, scratching madly at his blindfold.

Still holding the bowl, Eva opens the door. "Neena, what brings you by?"

"I was curious about that rabbit of yours," replies Neena, stepping into the cozy hut; the smell of muttonbird is strong. "Where is it, then?" Neena catches sight of the cage. "What an exquisite cage!" Then seeing the rabbit, she bursts out laughing. "Blindfold? You blindfolded the animal? Eva, surely you didn't take what I said seriously, about Adamos being reincarnated as a rabbit. Is it a girl rabbit that it wears a pink bow?"

At the sound of Neena's laughter, the rabbit becomes more agitated and begins charging back and forth, banging its head and body into the sides of the cage.

Neena sees the commotion.

"Look, Eva, the rabbit is acting strangely. What's wrong with it?"

Eva turns. "I don't know. Ever since I brought it home it has been acting up. Perhaps it misses its owners." She decides not to tell Neena about the rabbit sighing like Adamos.

Neena draws closer to the cage and lowers her face to the level of the rabbit. "What's the matter, rabbit?" she asks. "Your pretty bow's choking you?"

The rabbit screeches to a halt. *Bow? What bow?* Adamos realizes for the first time there is something tied around his neck. He would deal with that later. "You're the matter, Neena," he says with venom. "I don't like you. You're not welcome in my hut and you know that. What are you doing here now? Just being nosy is my guess. Go away." A paw shoots through the bars, just missing Neena's chin.

"You're aggressive, aren't you?" Neena pulls away slightly.

For a brief moment, the rabbit stands still, its instincts telling it that it is eye to eye with Neena. The rabbit draws a deep breath, its chest puffs out, its nose flares, its whiskers vibrate, and its lips seem to form the words. "GET OUT!"

"Huh!" says Neena, pulling back from the cage, her brown eyes open wide, for she is almost sure she has heard Adamos' voice coming from the lips of the rabbit. Neena stares dumbfounded at the animal and pushes a lock of her short, wavy, black hair behind her ear. The rabbit *is* Adamos.

"What's the matter, Neena?" asks Eva, observing her sister's unusual behavior.

I cannot tell her, thinks Neena. *It's bad enough I have frightened her into thinking the rabbit might be Adamos. But to tell her that I heard the voice of Adamos coming from the rabbit would only make things worse for her. No. This I cannot do. Perhaps it is my imagination. Yes, that's what it is, only my imagination.*

"This isn't a girl rabbit that it should wear a pink bow, Eva. Did you check?" Neena says instead, her mind working on a way to test the rabbit.

"I didn't put the bow on; it came that way."

"Have you any food, Eva? The rabbit must be hungry."

"But it won't eat the carrots and lettuce I put in the cage."

"I can see that, Eva. Have you any stew left?" asks Neena, curiosity banging at the door of her intuition.

"Why? Are you hungry?"

"Not for me, Eva, for the rabbit. Maybe the rabbit likes muttonbird stew."

"Don't be silly, Neena. No one feeds muttonbird to a rabbit."

"This rabbit might be different. Here, is there any meat left in your bowl?"

Reluctantly, Eva hands Neena the bowl containing one tiny piece of muttonbird. Eva watches as Neena grabs the morsel with her thumb and index fingers and carefully holds it against the side of the cage. Amazingly, the rabbit stops its erratic behavior, but its nose and whiskers still twitch madly.

Muttonbird, hmmm! Adamos savors the aroma. *And it's only inches away from my mouth.* He tries to resist the urge to let his mouth follow the smell of his twitching nose. *Resist*, thinks Adamos. *You don't want to eat from the hand of your enemy.*

Adamos forces himself to back away. His bottom jams against the back wall of the cage, but his nose continues the sniff the air. He digs his paws into the padding on the bottom of his cage.

If I play dead, Neena will give up, thinks Adamos. He flops onto his belly, his front and back legs splayed; the urge to crawl forward, still strong. He digs his front paws even deeper into the padding; spit trickles out the side of his mouth.

Nine

"Come and get it, rabbit," urges Neena. In her mind, she is thinking, *if the rabbit grabs the piece of meat, it will convince her that her theory about it being Adamos is right.* "Meat, rabbit, you know you want it."

"Neena," says Eva from the kitchen doorway, "don't tease the animal. Can't you see it has no interest in meat? Perhaps it misses its previous owner. That alone explains its peculiar behavior."

Meat? No meat. Meat? No meat, debates Adamos in his rabbit mind. He can restrain himself no longer and he lunges at the side of the cage, his instincts directing him to the meat Neena is holding. In one quick swipe, he grabs it and gobbles it with haste.

Eva sucks in her breath. "It eats like a greedy pig."

Neena studies the rabbit more closely. *You are Adamos, all right,* she thinks. *He couldn't resist muttonbird meat either. There's one way left to seal my conviction. I must see your eyes!*

Neena walks over to Eva and whispers in her ear, "Eva, do you mind if I remove the blindfold?"

"Neena, please, you mustn't … you still don't think that …."

"Indulge me, Eva; I merely want to see its eyes."

"It has eyes like any other rabbit, Neena, except for the color."

"Then why the blindfold?"

"Only me being foolish, Neena, that's all."

"Go to the kitchen while I have a peek, eh?"

"Suit yourself. But if the rabbit bites you, well, that's your problem." Eva picks up the empty bowl and with a backward glance at the rabbit, trots off to the kitchen. The rabbit, too busy licking its paws, has paid no attention to the whisperings of the two women.

With Eva gone, Neena returns to the cage and eases the door open. She grabs the unsuspecting rabbit by the scruff of its neck. The head remains rigid, but the rabbit's legs flick back and forth, seeking

59

firm ground. Neena plops the animal onto her lap and with her free hand, unwraps the blindfold.

"At last, Eva my love," twitches the whiskers, "you have seen sense enough to remove this silly blindfold. Oh my darling, how I promise to cha … Ye gads!" The blindfold falls free and Adamos finds himself staring into Neena's eyes. "YOU!" shouts Adamos, his rabbit mouth forming the words: "WHAT ARE YOU DOING HOLDING ME?"

"I knew it," whispers Neena, her face close to the rabbit's. "It is you! I can almost hear your voice, plus those eyes are a dead giveaway." She lowers the rabbit back into the cage. "You are trapped in there, aren't you, Adamos? I work with animals. I know their behavior. Rabbits don't eat meat, and from the way you grabbed the meat from my fingers, I knew it had to be you. Well? Are you in there, Adamos? Are you the rabbit? Slow down the twitching of your whiskers so I can hear you."

Adamos is confused. Neena is his number one adversary, yet it is she who now knows the truth about what and where he is. *Could it be the tree intended me to reconcile with my sister-in-law before I can be a man again? Of course, that's it. I figured it out! Any fool in my situation would draw the same conclusion,* thinks Adamos.

Convinced he is right about the solution to his predicament, Adamos knows what he has to do. He must make amends with Neena, make her his ally, and communicate with her, for she represents his only link now to Eva and ultimately to his becoming a man again. But how is he going to convince Neena he wants to repent and make Eva happy? He rubs his body against the side of the cage. With some effort, he heaves his rabbit body up to its full height, hooking his front paws around two of the bars. His hind legs strain to retain contact with the bottom of the cage. He makes an extra effort to slow the twitching of his whiskers.

"Of course it's me, you stupid woman. You're as thick as your sister, I tell you," says Adamos, pushing his rabbit mouth close to the wire framework.

"That's better, Adamos. Your coarse speech convinces me that you're in there." Neena smiles triumphantly.

"Good!" Adamos rubs his fat body against the bar, a plan formulating in his mind—he will use the enemy to facilitate his needs, but he must make an effort to improve his tone. His voice is soft when he speaks again. "Neena, you must help me. Take me back to the Great Pine, please."

"Why should I, Adamos? You despise me. Said so yourself."

"Yes, yes, yes, we both know that. Nothing has changed. All the same, you must take me back to the tree, for that is where my misfortune began." He could kick himself for lacking diplomacy. Blast!

"Your misfortune? Ha! You make me laugh, Adamos. Isn't it Eva's misfortune to be stripped of all her nuggets? And what about her confidence, eh? Even that you took away from her. Is it not Eva's misfortune that you treat her like rubbish? You dare talk about your misfortune. Where is your shame, Adamos? If you ask me, becoming a rabbit is too good for you."

"So you will not help me?"

"I see no reason why I should. The tree must have had its reasons for changing you into a rabbit. Perhaps you need to improve your stinking, lousy attitude. Perhaps you need to learn how to be kind, appreciative, and accommodating to your wife and to people in general. Perhaps you need to grow up. Perhaps you need a compassionate heart."

"Okay! Okay already!" shouts Adamos. "Take the bow off, then."

"No. It suits you." Neena and the rabbit lock eyes. She leans her head closer to the cage, readying to give Adamos a further piece of her mind. "Listen here, you piece of sh …."

"Ah! Neena, you seem quite taken with the rabbit," interrupts Eva with a laugh. "Take it to your sanctuary if you like. Maybe you are better able to help it reduce."

Neena pulls back from the cage. "No, Eva, I have no use for a fat rabbit with an attitude." Neena reaches for the rabbit again and, trapping its paws between her knees with more pressure than necessary, begins re-wrapping the blindfold around its eyes.

"No, Neena, no," pleads Adamos. "Not the blindfold. I hate the blindfold. I hate not being able to look at Eva. Listen, I promise to improve my attitude. Here, I'll prove it to you ... you're not as dumb as your sister ... what I mean is, I don't think either of you is really dumb. 'Tis only a joke I made, Neena, to ... to ... amuse myself. Take me back to the tree, please."

Neena laughs. "Eva," she says, "what a nice idea to blindfold the rabbit. I would keep it blindfolded all the time if I were you. It's bound to have some positive effect on its eating habits and attitude in general."

Eva laughs softly. "Tell me, Neena, did the eyes remind you of ... of Adamos?"

Neena coughs. Telling a lie is not going to be easy. She must be diplomatic. "Well, it depends. If you think of Adamos when you look at the rabbit's eyes, then of course you will think you see Adamos. But if you think of ...." Neena is having some difficulty thinking of another comparison. "If you think of me, for instance ...."

"I will think the rabbit reminds me of you?" Eva finishes, one eyebrow arches.

"Yes. That would be it."

"Somehow, I doubt it, Neena."

The sisters sit quietly, absorbed in their own thoughts. It is Eva who breaks the silence.

"Now that Adamos is gone I can get on with these repairs."

"Repairs? What repairs?"

"For months Adamos had been promising to fill the cracks in the walls and to patch the hole in the roof. It's always, 'Eva, get off my back. I'll fix them tomorrow.' Well, I waited for each tomorrow, only in Adamos' mind, tomorrow never came."

"You're much better off without the louse, that's for sure. Just think, Eva, think of all the things you can be doing."

"Like singing ... not cooking if I don't feel like it ... no extra clothes to wash and iron ... no underpants to darn ... no one telling me I have no brains?" asks Eva.

"Exactly!" Neena laughs. "Plus you can eat all the meat you like."

But listening to the women's conversation makes the rabbit restless again. *That Neena is trouble,* thinks Adamos.

"Look, Neena, look how the rabbit paces back and forth."

"Perhaps it finds all this talk about work unpleasant." Neena stoops in front of the cage. "Aren't you lucky, rabbit? You don't have to do anything but eat, sleep, and toilet."

"Hush, Neena. If you weren't so mean you would take me to the Great Pine, where I can become a man again and then I can help Eva with the repairs."

"Sure, like you've helped her before? You're all talk but no action, Adamos," whispers Neena. Then aloud, "I must go now, Eva."

"So soon? You've had nothing to eat."

"I'll eat at home. I only came to see the rabbit, remember?" Neena hustles towards the door, purposely ignoring the rabbit, which is banging its body into the side of the cage, begging her to take it back to the Great Pine.

"Goodbye, Neena." Eva hugs her sister.

"Bye, Eva. Good luck with the repairs and your new life ... with your new pet, which, by the way, is a MALE rabbit with a puny undercarriage."

"Neena, you didn't." Eva laughs.

"Yes, I had a look."

"Eh?" says Adamos. "You hussy!"

Eva stands at the door, waving until the darkness swallows her sister, before she returns to the rabbit. "Strange girl, my sister." Eva turns to the animal; it is busy pawing at the bow around its neck. "At least she's made you eat something, if only a piece of muttonbird. Perhaps you will eat the carrots and lettuce later." She stares at the animal, now crouched on all four paws, its fat belly pulsing like a bellows, its head swinging from side to side, as if it is choking.

"You look uncomfortable, rabbit. Is the bow around your neck too tight? Is that why you've been scratching at it?"

Adamos pushes onto his front paws, his whiskers tremble. "Yes, Eva. Free me from this girlie nonsense, for I am unable to detach it ...

then take the confounded blindfold off and return me to the tree."

But Eva quickly changes the subject. "You know, rabbit, Adamos doesn't like my sister. He would go ballistic if he knew she was here. I don't think Adamos likes anyone. Oh, he's good at pretending he likes someone, especially if it's a beautiful young girl fussing over him. But me? Anyone just saying hello to me makes Adamos cross … nasty cross."

"Say no more, Eva, please," Adamos twitters, raising his front paws to cover his ears.

Eva laughs. "I'm not surprised you don't want to hear any more about Adamos. That is why I prefer to go off during the day and help others. Being around Adamos only frustrated me. Nothing I did for him was ever good enough. There was much I wanted to share with him, but I knew we'd end up arguing, so I never bothered."

The rabbit presses its paws tighter against its ears. "Please, Eva, say no more. I'm sorry for all the bad things I've done to you, okay? I'm sorry I didn't listen more, okay? Now stop. I don't want to hear any more."

Oblivious to the tormented rabbit's pleas, Eva continues, "And there was the time when his own mother came to visit. Adamos treated her so badly, she left in the middle of the night, refusing to have Adamos walk her home."

"And it still haunts me," Adamos cries, and for the first time he is glad to have his eyes blindfolded. "Please, Eva, forgive me. I have been such A STUPID ASS. "

"What?" Eva stares at the rabbit. "I could have sworn I heard Adamos' voice say something about a stupid ass."

The rabbit perks up. "You … you heard that, my love? Yes, yes, it is I, Adamos, trapped in the body of the rabbit. PLEASE take this bow and blindfold off."

"There again … I heard his voice say 'please.' Adamos never says please, though." Eva sticks her index finger in her ear and jiggles it. "Silly me." She gives both ears a good jiggle. "Perhaps it's because I'm talking about Adamos that I imagine hearing his voice."

"Oh, what's the use," Adamos laments. "Even when she thinks

she hears my voice, her thick brain can't comprehend that it is I confined in the body of a fat rabbit. 'Tis only Neena who can help me, but she is a selfish beast."

"Will you not eat your carrots, rabbit?" asks Eva, her voice soft and gentle.

"Am I a rabbit that I should feed on carrots, woman?" Adamos forgets for a moment he is an animal. "Oh, confound it. I am a rabbit ... now, and I hate carrots. How I hate being a rabbit. Oh, my love, it's the punishment I deserve for being a donkey."

"Adamos always left me lettuce and carrots for my dinner," continues Eva. "He gobbled all the meat. Can you believe that, rabbit? Maybe that is why he grew so large."

"How many more times are you going to remind me of my deplorable behavior? Let it be, Eva my love, please. I'm tormented enough as it is."

Eva yawns. Tiredness begins to consume her. "I will go to sleep now, rabbit. Good night. Have a good sleep."

"Good night, my love. I'm sorry I cannot watch you sleep or hold you in my arms as I would have done once upon a time." Adamos tugs at his blindfold with his front paws. "I'll have to think of other ways to make you see I and the rabbit are one and the same – your Adamos!"

Ten

That night, Eva dreams of Adamos. *It is early morning. She and Adamos are on their way to help her sister build a low stone fence round her little hut. Suddenly, Eva remembers she has left her shoulder bag behind. "Adamos," she begins with uncertainty, for Adamos is in a foul mood as usual, "I ... I must return to the hut for my bag. Will you wait here while I run and get it?"*

"Wait here, Eva?" Adamos' face contorts with the rage he feels. "You've already wasted much of my time and you know how I hate having to do anything for your sister."

"I'm sorry, Adamos, were it not for lifting the heavy stones, I wouldn't have asked you. You go ahead, I must return for my bag."

Eva trots back to the hut. To her surprise, the door is open. "Just as well I came back," whispers Eva, cautiously stepping into the hut. The clanking of pots in the kitchen make her heart race. Eva inhales. "Who's there?" When no one answers, she tiptoes to the kitchen, poking only her head through the open doorway. Her eyes widen as she sees a young version of Adamos stirring a pot. A blanket wrapped loosely around his waist conceals his lower body. His upper body is bare of clothing.

"Adamos?" Eva's voice is barely above a whisper. "How can this be? I just left you on the road to Neena's. I don't understand."

Adamos turns and smiles tenderly at Eva, his eyes radiant with love. "I made us a lovely meat and carrot stew, my love." Adamos lifts the spoon from the pot and beckons for Eva to taste the stew.

This cannot be Adamos. Eva thinks. Adamos is fat and old. It must be a trick. This Adamos is so much younger and slimmer, just like he was when she first met him. Eva feels a warm glow consume her as memories of a once loving Adamos flood into her mind. Just as she reaches out to touch him, she hears a penetrating noise, like a handsaw grinding through timber. The dream ends abruptly.

A startled Eva wakes up. "Adamos?" she whispers. Sitting up, she looks around the hut for him. "Have you come back, my dear?" she speaks into the darkness. She still hears the loud, guttural snore.

Thinking Adamos has returned and is asleep under his blankets, Eva scrambles to her feet and lights a lamp. She follows the sound of the snores, which seem to emanate from the direction of the rabbit's cage. Eva staggers backwards; her jaw drops open, for it is the rabbit which is snoring.

"It is you, rabbit." Eva stares in shocked horror at the sleeping animal, sprawled on its back, its mouth wide open, its body jerking with every grinding utterance.

"You snore just like Adamos!" Eva says aloud, reaching into the cage and nudging the animal onto its side—as she has done many times to Adamos; and like Adamos, the rabbit gasps for air as if suffocating, turns, but does not wake up.

"Why should I be shocked? You are as fat as he is." Eva's next thought horrifies her. Maybe the rabbit is Adamos! The thought forces a loud "NO!" past her trembling lips.

Eva's shout wakes the rabbit. It stirs and tries to open its eyes, but the blindfold is too tight. "Was I snoring, my love?" twitches the whiskers, paws scratching at the blindfold. "I'm sorry. Now will you believe I am your Adamos?"

Eva watches the rabbit's front paws scratch madly at the blindfold. She shakes her head violently to clear her thoughts. "What you need is regular exercise, rabbit, like this." Eva flips the rabbit onto its back and begins to criss-cross and stretch the short legs. "Exercise is bound to stop you snoring when night comes."

"Whatever you say, my love." Adamos thinks Eva can hear him at last.

"I was having such a good dream about the Adamos I fell in love with—the kind, gentle Adamos, but you woke me up with your stupid snoring."

"I'm sorry, my love, but I will do whatever it takes to be the Adamos you fell in love with." Adamos stretches a paw towards Eva. "Please take me to the mountain, I beg you."

"I don't know why the Great Pine has lumbered me with you, rabbit. But the sooner you lose weight, the sooner I can get rid of you."

"Eh?" twitches the whiskers. "But it's me, Eva. I thought you realized by now." Adamos sighs at the hopelessness of his situation. "Oh, what's the use, my love, you still can't hear me. If only Neena would agree to take me back to the pine tree. Oh, what's the use?"

Eva hurries back to bed annoyed at the rabbit and half hoping she is able to recapture her dream. She blows the flame out. "Imagine me thinking the rabbit even snores like Adamos. I must stop thinking about him. That is perhaps why I keep sensing him in the rabbit. I'm being soft to think a large man can suddenly change into a small animal." Eva laughs softly. "It is absurd to think such a thing can happen."

"No, my love," replies Adamos, "it isn't absurd at all. I *am* your husband … your Adamos. I promise I'll be the Adamos I once was. I promise not to let my twisted thoughts and insecurities consume me again. Return me to the Great Pine and I'll beg for its mercy. Oh, but what's the use of all these promises? My darling Eva cannot hear me, and my confounded sister-in-law refuses to help me."

"Chubby rabbit. That's a good name for you," whispers Eva into the darkness. "From now on you're just a big, fat, chubby rabbit, nothing more, nothing less."

The rabbit covers its ears with its paws. Eva's words stab painfully at its heart. His situation is hopeless; his fate as a rabbit sealed forever. *Is there a reason to continue my existence?* Adamos ponders.

"Goodnight, Chubby, I hope I can get back to my dream." Eva yawns and flips onto her side. Within minutes, she is asleep, but the dream she so wants to recapture never returns.

Eleven

The following morning, Eva wakes earlier than usual. It is still dark, so she lights a lamp. Much has happened in the short time since Adamos' disappearance.

"How incredible," she mutters as she stumbles about drowsily. "It has only been one full day since Adamos left. I don't even miss him much. I feel as if … as if a huge weight has been lifted off me. That should come as no surprise, though. He treated me worse than a pig wallowing in mud. I'm beginning to like this new freedom."

Eva's mumblings stir the rabbit. It wakes just as she walks past its cage. "Is it morning already, MY LOVE?"

Eva falters, almost dropping the little lamp, for she is sure she heard Adamos say 'my love.' "Adamos … oh stop it, Eva," she scolds herself. "You'll drive yourself mad if you keep imagining hearing Adamos' voice. He's gone. Get that into your head. Good riddance to bad rubbish."

"No, my love, I'm not gone … I'm right here. I'm not bad rubbish, either. Oh, what's the use? How can I make you understand my predicament?"

Eva hurries into the kitchen. She puts a half-filled pot of water on the earth stove to boil for her bath, but she forgets to light the kindling. Then she gathers the tools she will need for the day's work. In her mind, she is thinking she will liberate the animal. She will remove its blindfold and allow it to run freely around the hut while she is at work. She will make herself look at its eyes and force herself to think that they are only rabbit eyes. This she must do to overcome Adamos' memory once and for all. She must stop seeing him in the animal.

With her new resolve, Eva returns to the rabbit's cage. She opens the little door and gently lifts the rabbit out.

"How soft and gentle your hands are, my love," coos Adamos,

twitching his mouth.

Eva takes the animal into the kitchen. With the rabbit resting comfortably on her lap, she begins to unwrap the blindfold.

"Ah! You're finally removing the blindfold, my love. That is a good beginning." Adamos sits patiently, allowing Eva to unwrap the strip of cloth. "How I long to look into your eyes, my sweet Eva."

"There you are, Chubby. You're free." Eva tries to push the rabbit off her lap, but it clings to her clothing.

The rabbit turns its face upwards, blinking rapidly as it fastens its eyes on Eva's face. "At last, my love, I can feast my eyes upon your lovely face." Its whiskers and mouth twitch simultaneously.

Eva quickly lifts her eyes away from the rabbit's upturned face. When the rabbit's cold nose touches her cheek, Eva springs up, sending the animal tumbling to the ground.

"I'll forgive you for that ... undignified descent," twitches the whiskers. "But even if you knew who I am, I doubt it would have made a difference, though."

"I'll get you fresh carrots and lettuce." Eva scrubs her cheek with the hem of her skirt and ignores the rabbit's glare and twitching whiskers.

Eva plucks off one leaf of lettuce and cuts four rounds from the end of one carrot. These she places on an old wooden platter. Turning around, she half bends to place the platter on the ground where the rabbit can get to it easily, but the rabbit is not where she left it. A disturbance at the table attracts her. The rabbit is perched on Adamos' favorite seat, thumping its right hind paw.

"The ground isn't good enough for you, Chubby?" Eva demands. "You snore like him. Your eyes remind me of him. Must you also sit on his seat? Get off! Hop it!"

The rabbit makes no attempt to move.

"I said, hop it ... scoot."

"Oh, my love." Adamos stares at Eva. "I'm doing my best to alert you to who I truly am. I am your Adamos. Can't you tell by now?"

Averting her eyes from the rabbit's, Eva plonks the platter on top of the table. "I will not fight with you as well," she snaps at the rabbit.

At the sight of the carrots and lettuce, the rabbit covers its eyes with its front paws. Eva grows impatient. "What is it now, eh? Carrots and lettuce not good enough for you? Well, that is all you're going to get. It's slimming food. Eat it."

But Adamos is thinking he needs to do one more thing to make Eva see he is the rabbit. He turns his rabbit head and stares unblinkingly at his favorite breakfast bowl.

Eva follows the rabbit's head movement. "Oh, no, you don't!" Eva breathes the words through clenched teeth. "Not his bowl as well. I shall smash it to smithereens. Just you wait." Angrily, Eva marches over to Adamos' breakfast bowl and picks it up. She hoists it over her head.

"No, my love," pleads Adamos, "you mustn't destroy my bowl. I merely want you to see that the rabbit is me." Adamos sighs. "Oh, what's the use? You cannot hear me. If only Neena wouldn't be so selfish. She is the only one who can help me now." Adamos closes his rabbit eyes, not wanting to see his bowl smashed. If only he could squeeze out some tears. He stands on his hind legs, resting his front paws prayerfully on the surface of the table.

Eva's arms swing down, but she does not release the clay bowl. Instead, she pounds it onto the table, inches in front of the rabbit's paws. "Blow!" Eva stares at the rabbit's tightly closed eyes and clasped paws. "Now it's praying. Oh, this is too much." She tips the carrots and lettuce off the platter and into Adamos' bowl. "Enjoy your breakfast, Chubby. If you really knew what Adamos was like, you wouldn't want to share his bowl."

Not bothering to finish her breakfast, Eva grabs her shoulder bag and storms out of the kitchen. She cannot believe what she has just said to the rabbit. "Shame on you Eva, you have let the animal get to you. It's only a stupid rabbit. You have to stop thinking everything it does reminds you of Adamos. He is gone. He might as well be dead. It is mere coincidence the rabbit behaves like him."

After slipping into her day clothes, Eva closes all the windows. She locks the door securely when she leaves the hut. A full day of voluntary work is what she needs. Once outside, she draws a deep breath. At the sight of the mountain, she frowns. "Why have you burdened me with a fat rabbit?" Eva stares at the summit, but is unable to see the tree from where she stands. "Have you any idea how irritating it is? Why couldn't you send it back to its owners? Guess I know the answer to that. They didn't want it. Well, neither do I." Eva braces her back against the hut, trying to stem the anger and frustration she feels towards the rabbit, trying to blot out the image of strangling the thing.

Deciding it best to leave her shoulder bag outside the front door, Eva dislodges herself from the hut and begins her slow climb up the mountain. In the quietness of the Great Pine, she will find some answers, and maybe, just maybe, she will convince the tree to take back the rabbit.

Twelve

Meanwhile, Adamos feels as if the silence inside the hut is pounding in his ears and clawing at him, trying to pull his soul out of the rabbit body he occupies, trying to tear him apart limb by limb for having been such a wretched husband. He stares remorsefully at the carrots and lettuce Eva has left for his breakfast and turns away in disgust. Accusing thoughts of his unforgivable behavior and attitude bombard his mind like thunderbolts.

Carrots and lettuce ... that's what you feed your wife, you mean miserable man. You claim to be intelligent, yet you behave like an imbecile. You treat Eva as if she is pig's muck. Shame on you, Adamos. You're nothing but a cowardly, spineless donkey.

Adamos covers his ears with his paws as if to block out the accusing thoughts.

It's no use doing that. The thoughts are inside your head. They are your own guilty thoughts. Blocking your ears will not stop them tormenting you. You need to change yourself, Adamos ... from the inside ... from the heart. Your future depends on you. You have to decide what happens from now on.

Adamos feels himself growing angry. But the thoughts are right. He must change. "But how does a stubborn man change from the inside? Tell me that!" He challenges his thoughts.

It's up to you to figure that out, Adamos, replies his thoughts instantly. *It's no good my telling you what to do. That's not how it works. You have to want to change.*

"I won't eat breakfast, for a start." Adamos jumps down from the stump, landing heavily on his paws. "Exercise! That's what I'll do, starting now." Adamos forces his rabbit legs into a slow trot around the small ground space in the kitchen then out to the main room. Round and round he trots between the two rooms. Each time he completes the circuit, he increases his pace. Adamos pants and sweats. Any desire to stop only acts as a spur to increase speed.

An hour later, Adamos can run no more. His legs ache and his mouth is dry. He collapses on the ground in the kitchen. "Water!" His pink tongue dangles from the side of his mouth. "Need water."

Adamos crawls along the ground looking for water. He looks up at the kitchen table then turns his head towards the tub, which serves for washing dishes. He could spring from the table to the tub. "Oh, I don't have the energy to jump that far just yet," pants Adamos, flopping his head onto his front paws. "I'll just rest a while, to slow my racing pulse."

Adamos thinks of Eva. "It takes so little to please my Eva, so little to make her laugh, so little to comfort her. Why didn't I spend more time listening to her instead of insulting her? Because I'm stupid, that's why." Adamos groans and shuts his eyes.

Exhausted, he falls into a deep but restless sleep.

Thirteen

Reaching the top of the mountain seems strenuous for Eva this morning. Perhaps it is because she feels guilty for keeping the nuggets in so accessible a place. Perhaps it is because of her restless night and thoughts of Adamos. Her heart is sad, not because of Adamos, but because she has failed to safeguard the precious nuggets.

At last, Eva stands before the entrance at the base of the giant tree. Semi-darkness still shrouds the island. The dew-soaked ground waits hungrily for the first rays of sunlight to dry the wetness. Eva inhales the fresh, moist air mixed with a hint of lavender and damp soil.

Eva enters the hollow and sits wearily on the familiar stump. Instantly, she feels the tree wrap its cloak of solitude snugly around her, lifting her sadness, willing her to trust her all to it. Eva closes her eyes; a smile of contentment and gratitude softens her face.

"You're so easy to please, Eva," says a voice.

Eva sighs lazily. "Why didn't Adamos see that?" she asks softly, her eyes prickle behind the closed lids.

"But he does," replies the voice. "Now."

Eva laughs. "Then why hasn't he returned? Why has he treated me in such a scornful manner? No, Great Pine, this time you're wrong. Adamos no longer cares about me."

"Not so, Eva, not so. I never make mistakes."

Eva shrugs. Her eyes remain shut.

"Will you believe me if I tell you Adamos is at this moment quite remorseful?"

Again Eva laughs. "What good is that to me? He has left and will not return." She opens her eyes and allows a single tear to slide down her cheek. She wipes it away with the tip of her index finger.

"Don't despair, Eva, all will be well in the end. You must trust me."

"So you know where he is?" asks Eva.

"In a manner of speaking, yes. But that is all you must know for the moment. Now, tell me, how is the rabbit?"

Eva stares long and hard at the ground in front of her, not quite knowing if she wants to talk about the rabbit at all, since talking about it is like talking about Adamos, and suddenly she just does not want to think or talk about either.

"Well, Eva? The rabbit. How is it?"

"I don't want to talk about it."

"Why not, Eva?"

"Because …!" Eva pauses.

"Because?" prompts the voice.

Eva opens and shuts her mouth.

"Does the rabbit annoy you so much that you cannot speak of it?"

Eva nods. "Yes," she manages to force past her lips.

"And why is that, Eva? Is it because of its weight? Does it still eat too much? What is it?"

"Can I bring it back?"

"Why?"

Eva realizes there is only one way to stop the questions. "I detest the rabbit … this particular rabbit. It snores like Adamos. It has eyes like Adamos. It sits on Adamos' seat waiting for breakfast. It wants its breakfast in Adamos' bowl …." Eva's body convulses and she bursts into tears. "It reminds me of Adamos," she finishes softly, wiping her tears with the back of her hand. "I thought I didn't care, but I do. Where is Adamos? Please tell me. I must find him."

"Don't cry, Eva. Listen, I will make things a bit easier for you. Fill your heart with love for the rabbit. Show it kindness. Talking to it about Adamos will ease your pain, and, surprisingly, help the rabbit reduce."

"Talking to the rabbit about Adamos will help it lose weight and ease my pain? That doesn't make sense."

"Eva. Have I ever misled you? You must trust me on this. I know what's best for you and the animal, too. I gave it to you, remember?

Do as I say. Talk to it ... show it love and compassion. Cuddle it sometimes."

The Great Pine has gone too far this time, thinks Eva. *Talking to the rabbit is one thing, but to love it ... no, it is preposterous. But who am I to argue?*

Eva feels more burdened as she climbs down the mountain and hopes her day of voluntary work with lift her burden.

Fourteen

Back at the hut, Adamos, sprawled like a stingray on the kitchen floor, is asleep from exhaustion. He dreams of four wooden platters set before him. On the first platter are a few thinly sliced pieces of carrots. On the second platter are finely chopped, luscious, green lettuce leaves. On the third platter are small chunks of assorted meat—boar, muttonbird, and fish. The fourth platter is full of shimmering water.

"Rise, Adamos ... rise and seek the sustenance you need. Eat or drink," says a voice in his dream. *"But you must only choose from one platter."*

Adamos twitches his rabbit nose, his tummy rumbles, and his throat is parched. He ignores the carrots and lettuce but stares longingly at the boar meat, his favorite. Adamos sticks out his rabbit tongue and tries to wet his lips, but even his tongue is dry.

"It's water I need most, but the smell of the boar meat stimulates my appetite. It isn't fair to test me so," Adamos complains. *"I'm thirsty, yes, but I'm hungry too. Water alone cannot sustain me."*

"Choose, Adamos, you do not have all day."

"What's the use? If I choose the meat, I will wish I had chosen the water. If I choose the water, I will wish I had chosen the meat. Take them all away. Let me starve and die from thirst."

"As you wish," says the voice.

Slowly, the plates and contents dissolve.

A sharp pain stabs Adamos' tummy, jolting him awake. Eagerly, he looks around for the four plates, before remembering he has only been dreaming. The dryness in his throat is real, though, and he finds it difficult to swallow.

Water! I must have water, thinks Adamos, looking longingly at the tub high above his head. *If I can spring up to the tub, I can have my fill of water. But, alas, I am much too fat to accomplish such a daring feat. If only Eva were here to help me.*

Adamos stares longingly at the tub again and tries to think of an innovative way of obtaining the much-needed thirst quencher. Perhaps he can spring onto the stump he uses for a seat, then he can climb onto the top of the table. From there he can make a mighty leap across to the tub. With that thought, Adamos pushes onto his paws. They tremble and cannot hold his weight. Adamos collapses to the ground. Regretfully, he realizes that in his weakened state, the task is impossible.

"Even if I could," whispers Adamos, "I might topple into the blooming tub … and drown … or I might bang my head against the side of the tub and knock myself out."

"So, are you going to just give up, Adamos?" challenge his thoughts.

"No." Adamos forces his lips to move. "Even though my limbs are weak and my head is aching, I must try one more time." He inhales a shallow breath, before forcing himself to stand. His paws are shaky, but he is determined to keep standing.

Adamos looks up at the stump he uses for a seat and shakes his head, for he is beginning to feel giddy. "Even my seat seems too high above my head. If only it wouldn't sway so much. Ah! I cannot do this thing. I am only a rabbit, not the man I used to be. I curse the tree for relegating me to this position. But I have only myself to blame for thinking I could safely hide there with Eva's nuggets. Oh, why did I even steal the confounded things? I have behaved badly and must now accept my punishment. Perhaps it is best if I should die."

Adamos resigns himself to defeat and allows his shaking legs to collapse under him. He plops heavily to the ground … only to spring up again as if he has sat on a sharp object. "What the … ?" he squeaks, for he has sat on something wet. "I suppose I must have peed myself out of frustration." He turns to look, and is surprised by what he sees. "Water! Where did that come from?"

The shock of seeing a bowl full of water temporarily paralyses Adamos, but his need for fluid overpowers him, and he laps noisily at the thirst-quenching, reviving gift, completely forgetting about his wish to die. The more Adamos swallows, the more he feels the surge of energy flooding through his body. He shudders, but keeps on lapping, his pink tongue flashing in and out rapidly, greedily. Finally, he has licked the bowl dry.

Satisfied at last, Adamos stretches his body, suddenly realizing how bloated and heavy he feels. Without a second thought, he mobilizes for another gallant run around the perimeter of the two rooms. If there is one thing he is determined to do, it is to lose weight and be a changed man for his Eva. Adamos looks down at his white fluffy paws, a cruel reminder of what he has become. He screeches to a halt, pondering his plight, wondering whether he is wasting his time.

When all is said and done, thinks Adamos, *I'm just a rabbit. What use will I be to Eva? What good is running if I'm to remain a rabbit for the rest of my life? Why did the tree have to deal me such a terrible hand? Why did I have to climb the confounded mountain in the first place? Nevertheless, rabbit or not, I must press on.*

Adamos breaks into a sprint, ignoring the splish-splash of water in his tummy. Soon the urge to pee overpowers him and he stops beside his old mattress. He spies a small gap leading to the mound of earth beneath the mattress—where he had temporarily hidden Eva's nuggets. "Perfect!" he whispers. "My own private toilet ... and Eva doesn't have to know about it!"

"Aaaaah!" Adamos groans with satisfaction after releasing what he thinks is a gallon of water. Now he is ready to endure another gallop around the rooms. There is no splish-splash of water in his tummy now. But Adamos does not pace himself, though, and soon begins to sweat profusely. This time when the need for a drink of water brings him to a halt, there is none to quench his thirst. Adamos feels giddy and collapses on the ground in front of the entrance to the kitchen.

"Eva! Help me!" he gasps, before slipping into blackness.

Fifteen

After a long day's work, Eva is at Neena's hut eating steamed catfish served on a bed of couscous. She is reticent. This bothers Neena.

"Eva, is something wrong? You haven't said two words since you arrived for dinner. Is it the rabbit?"

Eva sighs, lifting her eyes briefly. "Yes."

"But it's only a rabbit, dear." Neena is puzzled. "You've had one before ... and you loved it dearly, until it ..." Neena pauses, remembering how terribly distressed her sister was when the rabbit had died; how she had refused to eat for a whole week; how angry she was at the rabbit for dying. "Do you still wish Hoppippa was alive?"

"Having my Hoppippa back would be a blessing, but ... no, it isn't that which burdens me now, Neena."

Silence descends.

"So what is it then? What robs you of words?"

"'Tis the Great Pine. Making me custodian of this new rabbit is one thing. Now I'm to love the animal and show it compassion. I cannot do this thing, Neena ... not to this particular rabbit because ... it constantly reminds me of ...." Eva's voice trails off.

"It constantly reminds you of ...?" prompts Neena, knowingly.

"Him."

"Him? Do you mean Adamos?"

Eva nods.

"How so? Tell me, Eva." In the back of her mind, Neena recalls her visit to her sister's house the night before, when she conversed with the rabbit; when she discovered the rabbit is indeed Adamos. Has Eva discovered this, too? She must find out.

Suddenly Eva jumps up, almost tipping her stump over. "Oh, no!" she exclaims, eyes wide as she stares out the window, for she is certain she has heard Adamos say, "Eva, help me."

Thinking something outdoors must have startled her sister, Neena scrambles to her feet, her heart thumping at the suddenness of her actions.

"What is it, Eva? What have you seen?" Neena glues her eyes to the window also, but sees nothing, except darkness.

"It's Adamos, Neena. He's out there, at the hut even. He called my name. He needs me. I must go to him."

Before Neena is able to utter another word, Eva grabs her shoulder bag and rushes out of the hut, leaving her half-finished meal and cup of wild honeysuckle juice.

There is only one way for me to find out what's really going on with Eva, thinks Neena, *and that is to follow her.* Neena grabs a cloth and covers the food on the table. She can finish her meal later.

By the time Neena gathers her shawl and shuts the door to her hut, Eva is well down the path leading to her own hut. Neena pulls her shawl tightly around her shoulders, for the night air is cooler than she expects.

Eva mutters to herself all the way back to her hut. *Has Adamos really returned? Is he waiting at home for me? How could I have so clearly heard his voice?*

Reaching the door of her hut, Eva remembers to lift the mat. Even though there is no moon, something glows from beneath the mat. "Oh!" Eva curls her fingers around the cold, hard object. "It isn't solid like the others." She withdraws her hand. "It's round, yes, but has a hollow center." The tip of her index finger slips through the hollow center, and the cold object settles snugly around the digit. "Maybe it's a ring," whispers Eva, anxious to look at the object in the lamplight. She pushes open the front door with her hip.

"Adamos, have you returned?" Eva calls softly, dropping her shoulder bag beside the door, before lighting a lamp. When there is no answer, Eva sighs. "It was only my imagination. Adamos hasn't returned. How stupid I am to think such a thing." She remembers the ring on the tip of her index finger and examines it. "It's a ring all right, but why? What am I supposed to do with it? I don't need a ring." Holding the lamp in one hand, Eva hurries to the kitchen, intending to drop the ring into the cup behind the herb and tea leaves, before seeking out the rabbit. Just as she nears the opening to the kitchen, she stumbles on something soft.

"Rabbit!" she exclaims, looking down at her feet. Her eyes widen at the still figure of the rabbit on the ground. "Oh, no! It's dead." Eva's mind is in a whirl. Could it have been the rabbit calling to her for help? No! That is impossible. Animals can't talk. She dismisses the thoughts.

Eva plonks the lamp onto the ground and stoops beside the seemingly dead animal. Cautiously she reaches out and strokes the fluffy white fur, her eyes mist as waves of regret consume her for being uncaring to the poor animal.

"I'm sorry, Chubby." Eva forces back the tears. She lifts her hand to wipe a stray tear and sees the ring on the tip of her index finger. "It's my fault you're dead," laments Eva. "If only I had been more caring. If only I had loved you, instead of hating you. I know not why this ring was left for me, Chubby, but I want you to have it before I bury you."

Eva removes the newly discovered ring from her index finger, contemplating whether she should slip it onto the bow around the rabbit's neck. As she twirls the ring between her fingers, it suddenly separates to reveal a sharp tip. "It's an earring," cries Eva. "I can pierce your ear with it. Yes, Chubby, that's what I'll do. Even though it is only one earring, I will place it on your ear. No pain will you feel, for you are dead."

Singing softly to the rabbit, Eva presses the sharp tip of the earring through the rabbit's right ear. She is surprised at the ease in which it pierces the thin layer of flesh. Once the pointy end is through, it connects with the other end of the earring, forming a complete circle again. Eva sits back on her heels, puzzled, her eyes fixed on the "lifeless" rabbit.

"It's as if the earring was meant for you, beloved Chubby." Eva begins to sing softly, fighting back more tears.

Too weak to move, Adamos hears a faint melodious singing. He mistakes the source. "You have brought me a singing bird, Eva? Ah, that is much better than listening to your croaking …."

"How sorry I am that you are dead, rabbit. I will bury you tomorrow," Eva says aloud. "It's too late now."

"Eh! Bury me?" whispers Adamos weakly. "I'm not dead, my love."

"Bury what?" says Neena from the open doorway.

"Oh!" Eva scrambles to her feet as Neena walks towards her.

"You left the door ajar, Eva. What are you going to bury tomorrow?"

Eva looks down at her feet. "That. It's dead."

"What!" Neena drops to her knees beside the rabbit, her fingers fly expertly over the animal checking for signs of life. She leans her ear close to the rabbit's mouth.

"I'm not dead, Neena." Adamos' voice is weak, his rabbit whiskers barely move. "I might look dead, but I'm not. I can hear you."

"The rabbit is alive, Eva," announces Neena.

"It can't be, Neena. Look how still it lies."

"Weak … hungry … and thirsty, my love." Adamos tries to stick his tongue out to moisten his parched lips.

"Bring water, Eva," says Neena. "Hurry."

With a deep sigh, Eva hurries into the kitchen, returning just as quickly with a cup of water. This she hands to Neena. Helplessly, she watches Neena dip her fingers into the liquid and allows several drops to moisten the rabbit's parched lips.

"Lick, rabbit," Neena encourages. "Lick and revive yourself."

"It's no use, Neena," says Eva, wishing the rabbit would indeed show some sign of life. "Not even you can make a dead rabbit live again."

"Don't despair, my love," says Adamos weakly, but only Neena hears him. "A few more drops, Neena, but not on my nose, lest I inhale the fluid and suffocate."

"A few more drops, rabbit, and you promise to open your eyes, right?" Neena's voice is soft as she strokes the rabbit gently beneath its chin.

"Yes, yes." Adamos is irritated at the stroking. "And stop that blinking stroking stuff. Because I'm half-dead doesn't give you the right to be familiar. Stop that, now, or else."

"Or else what, huh?"

"I'll bite you, that's what."

"Really? You are not in a position to make such threats, rabbit." Neena chuckles. "Besides, what have you been doing to make you so exhausted?"

"Exercising."

"Exercising? No wonder you're half-dead. You've never done anything strenuous in your previous life to exhaust yourself, so why start now?"

"Well, it's never too late to start, dear sister-in-law, is it?"

"For you it is, Ad ... rabbit."

Eva bursts out laughing. "If it weren't so sad, Neena, I'd say you were actually conversing with the dead rabbit as if it really were Adamos."

Neena looks up and smiles at Eva. *If only you knew, sister dear,* she thinks privately, slipping her hand under the rabbit's soft belly. It is warm and soon Neena feels a movement as the rabbit tries to suck in air.

"It's coming to," announces Neena, her eyes gleaming in the lamplight. She lifts the animal to eye level.

Adamos slowly rolls his rabbit eyeballs under his closed eyelids.

"Look, Eva, look at the eyeballs. They're moving."

Eva sighs deeply, unable to voice her relief. She squats on the ground, beside her sister.

"What's with the earring?" asks Neena, noticing it for the first time. Before Eva can reply, Adamos fully opens his rabbit eyes. His vision is blurry but he tries to focus on Eva.

"Earring? What earring? Put me down, Neena," twitches the whiskers, its paw feeling for the offending object. "Get this girlie thing off me, Neena. It's bad enough that I must wear a pink bow. Must I be lumbered with an earring as well?"

Neena chuckles and plops the rabbit on the ground. "No can do."

On shaky legs, the rabbit staggers over to Eva, only to collapse beside her. Gently, Eva picks it up, placing it on her lap. The rabbit nuzzles its face in the folds of her skirt. Eva gently strokes its head.

"Ah, my love," mumbles Adamos, closing his eyes. "This feels much more comforting than your silly sister's touch."

"Talk about ungrateful," says Neena hotly, "I help you and that's all the thanks I get?"

Shocked at Neena's outburst, Eva glares at her sister, drawing the rabbit close to her chest. "You can't be jealous of an almost dead rabbit, can you, Neena?"

Jealous of Adamos? Neena thinks privately, staring at the rabbit. "No, Eva, I'm not jealous of this rabbit. I pity it. It will be some time before it can lose the excess weight it carries and so it will most likely have more episodes like this one. But I won't always be here to revive the stupid thing. You'll have to do it."

"And thank goodness for that. Your hands smell of dung anyway. My beloved Eva is all I need."

Neena bites her lower lip to stifle the words she wants to shoot at Adamos. A plan to test his sincerity formulates in her mind.

Adamos buries his nose against Eva's ample bosom. "This is where I belong, my love," he coos. "But what's the use? I'm only a rabbit now and your mean sister won't take me up to the Great Pine."

"You got that right," Neena bursts out before she could stop herself. Under her breath, she says, "It isn't the pine tree that turned you into a rabbit, Adamos, it is your own greed that did it."

"What have I got right?" asks Eva, puzzled.

Neena sighs. "You finally seem to care for the rabbit," stammers Neena. There seems to be no point revealing the rabbit's identity when little hope exists of Adamos becoming a man again.

"The poor thing," replies Eva, still oblivious to the fact her sister and the rabbit can communicate. "I don't understand why I suddenly feel sorry for it. Perhaps I might come to love it one day."

"That's the beginning, my love," sniffs Adamos. "It's only a matter of time before you and I can communicate again ... and I can love you as I once did."

Neena bursts out laughing. "Yeah, right! And I'm the moon, which brings light to Edengardenia. Face it, you only love yourself." Already she is thinking of a way to test Adamos' resolve to be a better husband, if he should have the good fortune to be restored as a man again. But her comments disturb her sister.

"That's a strange thing to say, Neena." Eva regards her sister with a frown. "You know how much I love and care about you …."

"Pay no attention to me and my mutterings, Eva." Neena walks briskly to the door. "I have an idea which will help you decide whether it is pity you feel for that pesky animal or the beginnings of genuine love and affection."

"Ignore her and her brainless ideas, Eva," pleads Adamos, glaring at Neena. "You do anything stupid, Neena, and I'll scratch your eyes out, first chance I get."

Sixteen

Eva is late getting out of bed the following morning. She foregoes her customary pilgrimage to the mountain and sets about preparing a small breakfast for herself, before filling Adamos' bowl with carrots and lettuce leaves. This she places in a corner of the kitchen floor, before fetching the rabbit from its cage. Eva deposits the docile animal beside the bowl, then settles herself at the table to enjoy a leisurely breakfast. She has forgotten about her newfound feelings for the rabbit.

A scratching noise alerts her to the corner where she has left the rabbit. To her amazement, it is nudging the bowl towards the table with its nose.

"What is it with you, rabbit? Must you start annoying me this early?"

"Annoy?" Adamos is shocked. "But last night I was your beloved Chubby, you were beginning to have feelings for me. Oh, my love, what has changed?"

"And stop twitching your whiskers. It makes you look like an idiot."

Adamos swallows the lump of astonishment in his throat. "Let me breakfast with you, my love," begs Adamos, as he brings the bowl to rest beside his old seat. "Perhaps then you will remember your feelings."

"Oh, I get it." Eva laughs. "You still think you're a royal rabbit and you want to sit on the table. Well, you're not going to annoy me today, so here!" Eva jumps up and hoists the rabbit and bowl onto the table. "Enjoy your food."

Eva picks up her wooden platter and cup and carries them to the other room. She will not compromise her dignity by having breakfast with a rabbit.

"Will you not eat with me, my love?" says Adamos, but Eva's

retreating back is his answer. Disappointed, the rabbit nudges the bowl towards the edge of the table until it tumbles to the ground and breaks. This brings Eva rushing back.

"Now look what you've done you silly animal." She half bends to gather the shattered bowl, but changes her mind. "No, I will not do this. I will clean up the mess when I'm ready. You can eat what's on the ground rabbit ... or starve. I don't care."

Adamos is hurt by this turn of events just when he was beginning to get through to Eva. *Perhaps it is my fault for trying too hard,* he thinks sadly.

Back in the main room, Eva finishes her breakfast. She surveys the repairs, which need to be done to the hut. Returning to the kitchen, she finds the rabbit sitting on its behind, its paws propped under its head, its blue-green eyes sad and dark. Eva ignores the animal and, grabbing an old bucket, heads outdoors.

Thinking that Eva has left for her day of voluntary work, Adamos sighs, disappointed that she did not say goodbye. "Have a nice day, my love." Adamos swallows the lump forming in his throat. "I'll look forward to your return this eventide."

Once outside, Eva quickly fills the bucket with a mixture of clay soil and dried grass. She returns to the kitchen and pours a small amount of water into the bucket, stirring it to thick, paste-like consistency.

The rabbit hops excitedly at the sight of Eva and settles down beside her right foot. "Oh, my love, you have returned! Perhaps you feel as I do ... depressed. How nice it will be for us to spend a whole day together. Oh Eva, my sweet, will you not pick me up in your arms and cuddle me against your bosom?"

But Eva has other thoughts on her mind. "That Adamos," she mutters as she stirs the contents of the bucket with unnecessary vigor, "always saying he would fix this and that, but the lazy beggar never shifted his backside to even start anything. I always knew I'd end up doing the repairs."

Eva's comments make the rabbit cringe. "Forgive me, my love." The rabbit buries its face in its paws. "Truth is, I saw no advantage in starting any project, for when I finish you would only find another for me to do."

When Eva moves, her right foot connects with the rabbit and sends it scrambling across the kitchen floor.

"For crying out loud, Eva," complains Adamos, leaving skid marks across the earth floor. "Don't you look where you're walking? You might have broken a rib or two." When Adamos comes to a stop, he stretches his body, but feels no pain.

"You stupid animal." Eva stamps her foot on the ground. "What are you doing hanging around my feet?"

Eva and the rabbit lock eyes. For a brief second she is lost in the depths of the rabbit's blue-green eyes, they were so much like Adamos'. "Ada—" She stops herself in time. Sucking in her breath, she hurries over to her shoulder bag. She must not allow her mind to trick her like this. She will force it to think of the rabbit as a stupid four-legged mammal.

Removing a short oval-shaped chunk of tree branch from her shoulder bag, Eva takes the bucket into the main room. She locates and fills all the cracks in the walls. Then she turns her attention to the potholes in the dirt floor. When all is complete, she pushes the table against the wall, climbs on it, and packs the mud mixture into the small hole in the thatched roof. Out the corner of her eye, she spies the rabbit, its head craning round the kitchen wall.

"You wish to help me, rabbit?" asks Eva with a tone of bitterness.

The rabbit bobs its head and twitches its whiskers. "That isn't the way to fix the roof, my love. When it rains the mud mixture will not hold."

"You can best help me by keeping out of my way," Eva warns, "unless you wish to be kicked clear to the summit of Fijora next time."

"Yes, I wish to return to Fijora, my love, but not by air transport." Adamos decides he will not exercise today. Guilt at seeing Eva cleaning and repairing the hut has drained all his energy. The least he can do is keep her company as she struggles with the work. He trots over to squat beside his bed, well away from Eva's feet.

Adamos is amazed at how Eva flits from one repair to another.

"How can you do so many things without breaking stride, my love? It is impossible." He feels dizzy.

When Eva begins to paste an assorted collection of shells gathered from the beach onto the walls, Adamos groans. His interest peeks when Eva forms round and square patterns with the shells— something she always wanted to do to make the walls pretty, but dared not while he was there.

"'The walls are fine as they are, Eva,'" she mimics Adamos. "'The place is jumbled enough as it is.'" Eva slaps the last shell into place. "Done! Only I should have done it long before now."

Adamos thumps his hind leg on the ground. "How was I to know the shells would make such a pretty pattern on the wall, Eva?" twitches the whiskers. "I just thought you had no idea what you were talking about."

Eva steps back to admire her handiwork. "How nice it looks. I should have ignored Adamos and done it years ago. He was so … unimaginative and … so controlling."

"How right you are, Eva. The walls look attractive, I admit. But unimaginative? No … I'm just practical and logical."

Eva continues with other repairs, and once she is finished, and the mud and grass mixture has dried, she sweeps the ground and brushes loose dirt from the walls. She cleans out the rabbit's cage and is puzzled that the padding is not wet nor does it smell as if the rabbit had been peeing on it. Nevertheless, she will wash and replace the padding. When Eva gathers Adamos' clothes and other belongings into two bundles, Adamos becomes agitated.

"THOSE ARE MY BELONGINGS!" Adamos forces the words past his rabbit lips.

"Adamos!" Eva spins around, for the voice she hears is without doubt his. "Have you … returned …?" Her voice trails off.

"I'm here, I'm here … I've always been here, my love." The rabbit hops up and down with excitement.

"Of course not, it's just my imagination playing games." Eva throws the rest of Adamos' belongings onto the bundles with more haste. She picks up his block of wild berry and tallow soap, along with his shaving knife. She sniffs the soap and utters a soft sigh. "I sometimes miss the smell of Adamos' shaving soap." Eva feels a sting at the back of her eyes, and she blinks to send it away. "Perhaps I will keep these two things, because … oh Adamos!" She stops herself from becoming too sentimental and risking a flow of unwanted tears. She ties up the bundles.

But Adamos notices. "You do miss me, don't you, Eva? And I … you. How I long to hold you in my arms and kiss away your tears."

"You know, rabbit, I carry a deep hurt from something Adamos did one year after we were married."

The rabbit's head shoots up. "Wh … what are you saying, Eva?" twitches the whiskers.

"Adamos had an affair with that … that … loose woman … !" Eva pauses.

"You … you knew about that?" Adamos is shocked.

"Only that rat Adamos didn't think I knew … but I knew … perhaps he's with her now …."

"No, my love, I'm right here, and I'm sorry about the fling with Jezebel. I was out of order. It was a moment of insanity on my part. Please, my love, forgive me," pleads Adamos. "Oh, what's the use?" Adamos groans and flops onto his mattress. He watches Eva haul the bundles outdoors.

Eva returns and stands beside Adamos' bed; the rabbit makes no attempt to move. "Well, the past is the past. Adamos is history," Eva says with conviction. "I don't care where he is, or who he's with. The sooner I get on with my life, the better." She reaches down and up-ends the mattress, sending the rabbit tumbling to the ground.

"Not again!" exclaims Adamos, remembering how he had unceremoniously toppled once before from Eva's lap. He hears Eva grumbling.

"What might this be?" Eva is saying, studying with astonishment the mound of disturbed soil where Adamos' bed has been. "It smells of pee and dung," she finishes, rubbing her nose.

A choking sound from the rabbit makes her look up. The rabbit's blue-green eyes bore into hers.

"Did you disturb the earth under Adamos' bed, rabbit?" asks Eva. "By the smell of it you were using it for a toilet, weren't you? Is that why you cringe in shame?"

The rabbit backs away. "I must have been sleepwalking when I did that," twitches the whiskers.

"That's it, isn't it? This is where you toilet."

"You really don't want to know the whole truth about that mound. It's where I buried the nuggets I stole. And yes, I've been using it to … er … conduct personal business." The rabbit turns and scurries off towards the kitchen. He will have to find new toilet facilities.

"You are one strange animal." Eva watched the rabbit scoot into the kitchen. She was half-tempted to chase after it and give it a swift kick out the back door. Instead, she quickly replaces the smelly soil with a fresh supply from the garden. She stomps on the new mound, flattening it level with the rest of the ground. She sweeps away any dribbles of loose dirt then props Adamos' bed against one wall, draping a clean blanket over it.

In the kitchen, Adamos investigates a new location for his toilet. He burrows behind the jars of herb and tea leaves and discovers a cup.

"What's this, then?" twitches the whiskers. Adamos hoists his body; his front paws hook over the rim of the cup. He peers into the cup, his rabbit eyes bulging. "What's this then? More nuggets? Eva must have decided to hide them here … in case I returned … Oh my love!" Suddenly the cup topples under the weight of the rabbit's paws and Adamos finds his head shoved snugly inside the cup. He wriggles this way and that, but the cup holds him like a giant suction; air supply is rapidly decreasing. He begins to hallucinate.

From the main room, Eva hears a persistent 'klonk-klonk' sound emanating from the kitchen. She hurries into the kitchen and is aghast to find the rabbit in such a predicament.

"So you steal, just like Adamos, eh?" Eva bursts out laughing. "Pity he didn't get *his* head stuck in the box when he tried to steal my nuggets." Eva hauls the stunned animal from the cup. "See what happens to nosy rabbits?"

Leaving the animal to recover from its near-death experience, Eva returns to the main room and busies herself once again. She works continuously, stopping only to use the outdoor toilet and to swallow a small cup of boiled water. Soon the entire hut is transformed and she is pleased.

Thinking of the rabbit's needs, she fills a wooden tray with dirt and places it on the ground, not far from its cage. "This is where you will toilet, rabbit," she says aloud.

Adamos, still recovering from his ordeal, peeks out from behind the kitchen wall. He sees the tray. "It's not private enough." He hesitates. "But it doesn't matter. I've found my own place." He settles beside the tree stump that is his seat, disappointed that Eva has shown so little concern.

Eva makes one last check of the two rooms to ensure there is no more work to be done. "Finished at last." Eva wipes her brow with the back of her hand, then bursts into song, her voice in crescendo.

Adamos' ears stand at attention. "The singing bird ... it has returned. Oh, how beautiful it sounds." Adamos inches towards the doorway, and not wanting to frighten the bird, cautiously pokes his head out, his eyes searching, searching, searching, but all he sees are Eva's lips moving.

"Eh!" Adamos' rabbit eyes bulge out of their sockets. "The singing bird is Eva? This cannot be." Adamos vigorously rubs his eardrums in a mad attempt to dislodge the veil, which gives Eva's voice a melodious touch. But even that doesn't help, for the rapturous sound continues and so does the movement of Eva's lips. Adamos plops onto his belly ashamed that he never really appreciated Eva's voice before. "Oh, what an ass I am!"

"At last I can relax and enjoy my surroundings." Eva slumps on a stump, but her moment of relaxation is short-lived, for there is a sudden pounding on the door.

"Who can that be?" She hurries to the door. But before she can open it, Neena bursts in.

"Eva? Are you all right? No one saw you about today ... oh, how nice the place looks."

"My dear, Neena, I spent the entire day repairing and cleaning. I've done the lot. Sorry if everyone was worried."

"You missed all the excitement down at the beach."

"Excitement?" Horror replaces the joy in Eva's eyes. "Have they found a drown body? Is it Ada—?"

"Nothing like that, Eva. A huge black marlin washed up on the beach. We tried to push it back out to sea, but it died. 'Tis a delicacy, Eva. Here, I brought you a good chunk of its flesh. Have you eaten?"

Eva sighs with relief before answering. "Not much, Neena; didn't want to stop to do that."

"Then you must be famished."

"I am, dear, but that's all right. I will have bark tea and pancakes."

"Cook the fish, Eva ... all of it. But don't eat until I return. I've been working on a surprise for you this day. Make sure you're washed and dressed. I'll be back in half an hour."

"Neena, wait ...," begins Eva, but her sister has already dashed out the door. Truth is, Eva does not want to keep or cook the chunk of fish, because it is another of Adamos' favorites.

But Neena is fully aware of this fact. She just cannot believe her luck. The very day she plans to put Adamos to the test, his favorite fish washes ashore. How ironic!

Seventeen

The time has come to carry out her plan. Neena runs from her sister's hut, stopping only when she reaches the place where Cora, Bess, and Dahlia—some of Eva's long lost friends, are already waiting.

"Come along, girls." Neena beckons. "Eva has not been sick this day. She's only stayed in ... to give her hut a good cleaning. Come, she's waiting."

"Is she expecting us?" Cora hesitates.

"And what about Adamos?" Dahlia folds her arms across her chest. "He hates me. That's why I've kept away from Eva's hut these many years."

"Me too," joins in Bess. "This isn't a good idea, Neena."

"Don't worry about Adamos. He's ... not around."

"Might he not return while we're there?" asks Dahlia.

Neena takes a deep breath. "Trust me, he won't. Come, let's be going. Eva will be happy to see you. She has a new rabbit. She will want you to see it."

Meanwhile, back at the hut, Eva has returned the rabbit to its cage. She has prepared steamed marlin, and boiled an assortment of vegetables. Now washed and dressed in clean clothes, she waits for the familiar pounding on the door. She does not have long to wait.

"Ah, Neena ...!" she begins, pausing mid-sentence when she sees her three old friends behind her sister. "Oh my!"

"Here we all are, Eva." Neena pushes past her sister, her eyes searching for the rabbit. Good, it's right where she wants it to be for her little experiment ... but it's asleep. She sniffs the air and thinks, *Ah! Eva has cooked the fish.* "You remember your old friends, don't you, Eva?" Neena speaks loud enough to wake the rabbit. If the rabbit has heard her, it makes no attempt to show it. Neena jiggles the cage. "You remember Dahlia, Bess, and Cora." She lifts one end of the cage slightly then drops it with a thud. Still the rabbit does not wake.

"Neena, I heard you the first time," replies Eva, assuming Neena is speaking to her. "Of course I remember Dahlia, Bess, and Cora. But why wake the rabbit?"

"It would be good for your friends to see how active it can be," replies Neena, shaking the cage again. "Wake up, rabbit; I've brought you some visitors. Here, Dahlia, look at the rabbit."

Dahlia brings her face close to the cage. Neena rattles the cage. The rabbit's eyes pop open and lock onto Dahlia. The rabbit springs forward, crashing into the wall of the cage. "Yikes!" Rabbit spit spews from its mouth.

"The stupid thing just spit in my eye," complains Dahlia, pulling back and wiping her eye. "A bit wild, isn't it?"

"Serves you right," yells Adamos. "Who invited you here anyway?" Then seeing Neena, he says, "Oh, don't tell me. You brought her here, didn't you, Neena?"

"Yes." Neena simultaneously answers both Dahlia and Adamos. "It's a feisty and positively stupid rabbit, don't you think, girls?"

Just then, Adamos spots Bess and Cora. He becomes more agitated and begins charging back and forth in the cage. "Get out! Get out, all of you. None of you is welcome here. Get out!" Adamos is livid.

Neena leans close to the cage; Adamos draws to a halt in front of her. "I knew it," murmurs Neena between clenched teeth. "All your talk about feeling sorry for the way you've treated Eva was nothing but lies, wasn't it? Admit it. You're nothing but a lying ...."

Adamos brings his rabbit nose close to Neena's. "Get out of my hut and take those vagrants with you!"

Dahlia bursts out laughing. "Neena, if I didn't know better, I'd say you and the rabbit were having a serious argument."

"Perhaps I should cover the cage." Eva reaches for a blanket.

"No, Eva ... don't be hasty," says Neena, shielding the cage. "The rabbit needs exposure. It will help it become more ... er ... adaptable."

"Adaptable?" Eva raises one eyebrow. "To what?"

"People, Eva," replies Neena, moving aside. "See how frightened it is by your friends? Trust me, Eva, it will do the thing good in the long run, you'll see."

Adamos throws his rabbit body hard against the cage; his breathing heavy. "Me frightened, Neena? Of them? You have to be joking. I don't like Eva's so-called friends. And as for you, I'll scratch your eyes out first chance I get ... of that I am certain. Just you wait."

"It huffs and puffs like a bellows. It could give itself a heart attack," says Dahlia.

"And put it out of its misery," agrees Neena, lifting one end of the cage and letting it drop with a thud.

"Oh, what's the use?" says Adamos, flopping down on his tummy. "Why should I provide the entertainment?"

The women gaze with amusement at the rabbit.

"It's good Adamos is away, isn't it, Eva?" says Dahlia. "How peaceful the hut feels without his grouchy presence."

Eva inhales deeply. Did they know Adamos is gone for good? She looks questioningly at Neena, who, reading the uncertainly in her sister's eyes, shakes her head slightly. "Yes, 'tis good he is away," answers Eva with some hesitation.

"Gives us a chance to catch up on the years we've missed," pipes up Cora. "It will be nice to laugh and joke freely with you again, Eva."

"He had no right keeping us apart these many years." Bess purses her lips. "We knew each other long before he came into the picture."

"You're right, of course, girls," replies Eva, tempted to tell them about Adamos absconding with her treasured possessions. Instead she says, "Hungry, girls? I have steamed marlin soaked in passion fruit juice and seasoned with herbs and spices. You interested?"

"Oh, yes we are," Neena butts in. "Let's have it here. That way we can keep the rabbit company. Pity Adamos cannot enjoy his favorite fish."

"You're hateful, Neena," groans the rabbit.

"I know." Neena looks at the rabbit.

"Let's eat outdoors, it's such a lovely evening," suggests Eva.

"It's better in here, sister dear," Neena insists. "Come, we'll help."

Neena and the others follow Eva into the kitchen. Moments later, they return with steaming bowls of food. The aroma permeates the air.

"Let's sit at the table," suggests Neena, sitting next to the rabbit's cage.

It is a tight squeeze, but all the women fit around the table, adjusting their behinds to fit comfortably on the tree stumps used for seats. The smell of fish is intense; Adamos' rabbit nose twitches madly. "Blast all of you." He turns his back on the gathering. "And you, Neena, you're spiteful for flaunting marlin in my face. You are most hateful."

"I know." Neena blows fish breath into the cage.

"Well ... what do you know?" asks Cora.

"Us ... together like this ... is good for Eva," stammers Neena, plunging her spoon into her bowl.

"I really dislike you, Neena." Adamos grips a bar.

"I know," says Neena.

"You already said that, Neena," says Cora.

Neena laughs, but her ear catches a desperate plea from Adamos.

"Neena, at least tell Eva I'm here and not with ...."

"Her! You rotten, cheating ..." says Neena aloud.

"You knew?" twitches the whiskers.

"What is wrong with you, Neena?" Eva is alarmed at her sister's outburst.

Neena laughs. "I'm fine, Eva, but I think it's time your rabbit had a mate."

"A mate!" exclaims Eva. "Oh no, Neena! A mate will only mean more work ... rabbits breed like ... rabbits."

The women break into peals of laughter.

"You can always have the male neutered." Neena eyes the rabbit with disdain.

"Neutered! But, Neena," begins Eva.

"I'll have *you* neutered first, Neena," groans Adamos.

"Yeah, right," says Neena to Adamos, then to Eva, "I can easily do it, Eva—snip, snip with a sharp pair of whalebone scissors; dead easy. No trouble at all."

This brings more peals of laughter.

"Like heck you will, Neena." The rabbit crosses its back legs.

The women finish their meal, but remain at the table chatting. Neena spies the wooden tray of dirt on the ground. "What's with the tray, Eva?" Neena points with her chin.

"That's for the rabbit to use for ... you know ... its needs."

Neena laughs. "You mean it needs a special place to pee and ...."

"Yes, Neena," Eva interrupts.

"What's wrong with doing it in the cage?"

"I prefer the tray, Neena. It's much easier for me to clean. I merely have to replace the soil," says Eva.

"Is Adamos going to be gone long, Eva?" Dahlia butts in.

"Ah ... well ..." stammers Eva, searching for the right words.

"Adamos is on a personal pilgrimage, Dahlia," Neena jumps in.

"He could well be gone a long time," adds Eva.

"Good," says Bess. "We can meet every week then."

All this talk about toilets and Adamos' whereabouts cause a build up of gas in the rabbit's tummy. A wicked thought springs into Adamos' mind. *If this doesn't get rid of you lot, nothing will.* Revenge is sweet. Adamos releases the gas. Silent, but deadly! He turns his head slightly to enjoy the reaction. *One ... two ... three ...!*

Neena jumps up. "You are one rude, disgusting rabbit." She presses her hand across her nose.

"I know," twitches the whiskers.

"Time we left," says Dahlia politely. "Goodbye, Eva."

The women make a mad dash for the door, holding their noses. Eva waves goodbye. Because she is a bit tired, she is not sorry to see them go, though the manner in which they leave annoys her.

"Did you have to disgrace yourself so?" Eva reprimands the rabbit.

"Yes, my love. And I'm not sorry. If you have any sense, you would shut them out of your life ... your sister included."

Eva makes no further fuss with the rabbit, but washes the dishes and tidies the hut before settling down to sleep. The rabbit paces restlessly in the cage.

"What's the matter, Chubby? Feeling guilty about what you did?"

"Why did you let them in? I DON'T LIKE ANY OF THEM!"

"What!" exclaims Eva, spinning around to face the door. "I thought I heard Adamos' voice say 'I don't like any of them.' Perhaps Adamos is dead and his spirit is haunting me again ... he must be here ... his soul is restless ... be gone, you restless ghost of Adamos. You're not welcome here anymore. This is my hut now ... to do as I please."

"But, my love, I've been trying to tell you I'm here. I'm the bloody rabbit, not a ghost ... and I *have* changed."

"Ghost of Adamos, listen well," Eva continues, "you have no power over me now. No longer will you control my life. No longer will you be able to damage my self-confidence with your stupid insults."

The rabbit repeatedly bangs its head against the bars.

"If your ghost eyes can see me now, Adamos," continues Eva, noticing the agitated rabbit, "you'll discover I am capable of coping without you. Look at the rabbit. Talk of you disturbs it. So go haunt yourself. And one more thing, ghost, my friends are welcome here anytime and there's nothing your ghostly form can do about it."

Adamos crumbles to the bottom of his cage and claps his front paws against his ears. "Oh, what's the use? 'Tis useless ... a rabbit I am ... a rabbit I will remain. I must return to the pine tree and plead with it to take my life ... no, that is the attitude of a defeatist and a stupid way to think. I will not accept defeat, just yet. I'll continue to improve my ways, then I'll beg the Creator to make me a man again."

"Perhaps Neena is right," Eva says aloud; the rabbit's ears perk up. "From the beginning, she said I should find a new husband. Perhaps it is time. Perhaps a new husband will chase the ghost of Adamos away forever."

"A new WHAT?" Adamos shudders, his rabbit nose flares, and his front paws grab the bars of his cage.

"You heard, ghost of Adamos. Yes, a new husband should force you to flee once and for all to the world you now belong to."

Eva's revelation seals Adamos' resolve. He must devise a way to seek audience with the Creator. *I am the only new husband Eva must get. Of that I am convinced.*

Eighteen

For the next few weeks, Adamos is more focused. Each day he continues to race around the hut soon after Eva leaves for her voluntary work. He recites a mantra: *I am kind and patient … love and affection every day for my Eva, come what may.* He eats only when he is hungry, drinks water only when he is parched.

Adamos knows his efforts are paying off because he groans less and less when he runs. He feels much slimmer around his waist and he is able to hop higher and higher. He feels his rabbit body becoming stronger and his legs more muscular and powerful. Amazingly, however, the bow self-adjusts to fit snugly around his neck.

Adamos finds Eva's friends less and less annoying each time they come to the hut for a meal and a chat. Talk about him assists in improving his attitude. He remains determined to stay focused, even though Neena continues to pester him.

Then one evening, after Eva returns home, she finds the rabbit perched on top of the kitchen table. "Oh, my." She strokes the rabbit's belly. "How agile you have become. I can no longer call you Chubby now, can I?"

The rabbit blinks rapidly at the sound of her voice and the touch of her hand. "Thank you for the compliment, my love." The rabbit wriggles its body in response to Eva's caress. "And I did it all for us. Take me to the mountain, Eva. Perhaps this night I can be your loving husband again, if you know what I mean."

"I don't know how you managed it, rabbit, but you have lost a fair amount of weight. That is good. I'm proud of you. Now I can return you to the Great Pine."

This makes Adamos happy. He springs up onto his hind legs, pawing the air with his front paws. It is what he has wanted for a long time now. "Yes, yes, my love, take me back to the tree so I can become a man again."

Eva picks up the rabbit and returns it to the cage. "Funny thing," she says, an unexpected lump forms in her throat. She struggles to understand her sudden attachment to the animal she so disliked at first. Unknowingly, she has allowed it to become part of her.

"What? What? Funny thing what?" prompts Adamos, his whiskers twitching madly.

Eva clears her throat. "Funny thing is, I don't really want to send you away now, rabbit. I've grown accustomed to you. Perhaps, in the morning, I will tell the Great Pine I now wish to keep you."

Adamos props himself up on his hind legs. His front paws wave feebly in front of Eva's face. "No, no, my love," twitches the whiskers, "you must take me back to the tree ... the Great Pine ... tonight."

"It could be because I can talk to you ... you know, tell you things ... makes it easier for me to deal with what Adamos has done," continues Eva, oblivious to the rabbit's turmoil. "And you listen ... you do not hush me up like Adamos would do ..." Eva pauses.

"Yes, my love, not only have I been listening ... I am ashamed of the things I've said and done. I will no longer say you make no sense when you speak. Okay, I will no longer pretend I'm deaf when you try to tell me something that is of no interest to me. The mountain ... please."

"... Like the time I asked him to explain how Edengardenia and its people came to be. The way Adamos glared at me; you'd think I'd asked him to fetch the moon."

"Stop, Eva, say no more ... just take me to the damn mountain."

"I believe he didn't know the answer," continues Eva. "So instead of admitting it, Adamos shouted, 'I don't understand a word you're saying, Eva.' You'd think he didn't understand my language!"

"No more, Eva ... I've been a real donkey's backside all these years."

"Adamos was always putting me down in front of others," Eva went on, "so it came to a point where I just didn't want to go anywhere with him, not if there were people there that I knew. Adamos liked to embarrass me when he had an audience. It made him feel in control, I guess."

The rabbit groans. "No more, Eva, please. I'm a changed man now and I love you so much. Please return me to the Great Pine."

What Eva says next sent shock waves through Adamos' body. "You know, rabbit, I think Neena is right. If I keep you, I will ask the Great Pine for a mate for you. You would like that, wouldn't you, rabbit? But I warn you, you'll have to be neutered."

Adamos gives his rabbit body a violent shake, almost shifting the cage a full inch. "A rabbit mate? Neutered? No, Eva … I am a man … you are my mate. I don't need a rabbit. Blast that Neena for planting that stupid idea into your head. I need you, Eva. Take me to the mountain before you do something we'll both regret."

Unfortunately, Eva does not understand or even hear the pleadings of the rabbit. Instead, mistaking the rabbit's antics for hunger, she reaches into the cage and picks it up. "Ah," she whispers, blinking back her tears, "are you hungry?"

"No, no," Adamos pleads. "I don't want any blinking food. I want to go to the mountain." Adamos squirms against Eva's chest.

"Don't fuss so, rabbit." Eva strokes the fur. "I'll make you something special for dinner, as a treat for being such a good rabbit lately."

"Oh, what's the use?" laments Adamos, perched on Eva's shoulder. He presses his cold nose against her ear. "If you can hear me, my love, this I promise, I will not eat dinner. I will not eat again until you take me to the mountain."

Eva returns to the kitchen balancing the rabbit on her shoulder. When she bends to put the rabbit on the ground, she notices the lettuce and carrots remaining in the bowl.

"You haven't eaten much today. That explains why you're so agitated. You're hungry. So am I. I'll fix us dinner." Eva lifts the rabbit off her shoulder and puts it on the ground.

"Oh, what's the use?" Adamos lays his head on his front paws and closes his eyes. "It's not food I want, my love … it's you."

Eva has no meat left. She will make a small portion of vegetable soup. She half-fills a pot with water and adds to it chunks of carrots, cassava roots, and tomatoes. She spices up the mixture with herbs. When the cassava roots soften, Eva crushes a few to help thicken the soup. When the soup is finished to her satisfaction, Eva places a small amount into a bowl and places it beside the rabbit. She is alarmed because the rabbit's head is drooped to one side; its body stretched out limp and lifeless.

"What is it? Are you unwell? Oh no! You must have done yourself harm losing so much weight. What shall I do?" Eva stoops beside the rabbit and strokes behind its ears. "I must get Neena." She scrambles to her feet.

Adamos' head pops up. "No! Not her! Don't get her. She might have me neutered just for the hell of it." His eyes plead, but Eva is already racing out of the kitchen and does not see that the rabbit is alive and well. "Please don't get that miserable, scissor-happy, gender-altering sister of yours." Adamos chases after her.

"Neena will help you," Eva mutters, her feet hurrying towards the lit lamps. Adamos scurries behind her, a plan beginning to formulate in his head.

"Like heck she will," groans Adamos.

Eva blows out the lamps and in the resulting darkness opens the front door. Not far behind is the rabbit. Eva steps outside. So too does the rabbit, instantly crouching under the shadow of a low bush. The rabbit watches Eva charge towards the main road. After a good ten minutes, it sniffs its way down the path, its eyes fixed on the gigantic mountain high above its head.

Only one thought pounds in Adamos' head: he must reclaim his manhood, and he must do so ... this very night!

Nineteen

Adamos strains his eyes to see through the darkness to make sure Eva is well out of sight. He turns to the mountain. "I have unfinished business with you, Creator of all that is." He begins a slow hop as he speaks.

At the bottom of the enormous mountain, Adamos hesitates. "This is going to be tough going." He inhales deeply. "I hated climbing this thing as a man and I'll certainly hate climbing it as a rabbit. But climb it I must. This time though, I'll use the rugged path."

Adamos is surprised how agile he is springing from rock to rock. His breathing is easy and soon he finds the experience exhilarating.

"I shouldn't be so surprised at my agility," says Adamos, pleased with himself. "My former body was way out of shape. It just goes to show how a little exercise can be beneficial."

It doesn't take Adamos long to reach the summit. Slightly winded, he stops to draw air. "Fit or not, anyone is bound to be breathless after such an arduous climb." He draws another deep inhalations.

After a few more deep breaths, Adamos seeks and finds the entrance to the base of the pine tree. He pokes his head in to make sure he is alone before he springs onto the stump used as a seat.

"So, you've come on your own I see … and looking quite fit, too," says a voice, which seems to come from directly in front of Adamos.

Adamos twitches his rabbit whiskers. His mouth feels dry and he has to cough to clear the constriction in his throat. He should have spent some time preparing his plea.

"What choice did I have?" he asks with hesitation. "That stupid sister-in-law of mine flatly refused to bring me before."

"And what is it you want that couldn't wait 'til morning, Adamos?"

"As if you don't know!" Adamos pauses, contemplating whether his approach should be brash or humble.

"What is it I'm supposed to know, Adamos?"

"That Eva talks of neutering me and finding me a mate ... a rabbit mate for goodness sake."

"So?"

"So? So! How would you like to be neutered, eh?" Adamos feels his temper rising and knows that he must control it. He takes a deep breath to simmer his emotions. "Please, your Worshipfulness, I don't wish to argue." He tempers the tone of his voice. "May I be a man again? May I be given a second chance?"

"Ah ha! So you wish to become a man again, is that it?"

"Yes. I believe *that* is what I asked," replies Adamos, swallowing rising anger.

"Isn't Eva giving you the attention you sought as a man?"

"Yes, yes, she is ... as a rabbit, yes ... but ...."

"You hesitate, Adamos."

"Give me a second chance at being a man, please."

"So you can make another *wife* miserable?"

"Another wife?"

"That's what you said you were going to seek. Surely you remember ... an obedient wife ... you said."

"No! No! No! I seek no other ... only Eva. Please change me into a man again ... I ..."

"And why should I do that, Adamos? What makes you think you deserve that privilege again?"

Adamos bows his rabbit head, assuming a posture of defeatism. He can think of several reasons why he should become a man again. As a rabbit, it is impossible to show Eva proper affection. As a rabbit, it is impossible to tell her how much she means to him. As a rabbit, it is impossible to cook the delicious meals he remembers preparing for Eva when they were first married. Yes, he wants to be a man again to correct all the wrongs he has done to his beloved wife. Adamos sighs deeply.

"Just let me have a second chance, O Gracious Majesticness," begs Adamos, a quiver in his voice.

"Why? So you can make Eva's life miserable again? Isn't she much happier since your unfortunate disappearance, Adamos? You tried to break her, remember?"

"Okay! Okay! I admit I have miscalculated Eva's strength. I admit I have been a rotten, stinking rat … er … rabbit … er … man …! I admit I don't deserve a second chance with my Eva, but how cruel can you be?" snaps Adamos.

Adamos feels suddenly hot. He jumps off the stump and charges about like a rabid animal. "You can't do it, can you?" challenges Adamos. "You call yourself the Creator of all, yet you don't have the power to do it, do you? Then tell me who can so I may seek him."

"Temper! Temper!" says the Creator. "That much has not changed. Just as well Neena didn't bring you back here before. Sounds like you still need time to improve."

"No! I have changed, I know I have," pleads Adamos. "I'm merely frustrated. I just need to be normal again, for Eva's sake … for my sake then. Will you … can you do it?"

"What makes you think that, as a man, you will be any different towards Eva?"

The words strike Adamos like a blast from a shotgun. He screeches to a halt and jumps onto the stump again. He stares at the wall. He opens his mouth to speak, but quickly shuts it again. He lowers his head. "Perhaps you are right, Great Creator. Perhaps I can only show my affections as a rabbit. Pardon my earlier insolences. Perhaps I'm not yet ready to be a man again, let alone a husband to my Eva." Adamos pauses, his breathing is heavy, and his eyes are misty. "What's the use? A rabbit you've made me … a rabbit I will remain. Just don't send me a rabbit wife. Celibate I shall remain for the rest of my existence." Adamos jumps off the stump and charges towards the exit.

"Running away again, are you, Adamos?"

Adamos halts. He looks over his shoulder. "I'm not running away, Your Greatness," he says softly. "I'm just going back to the hut … before Eva returns. She'll worry if she finds me gone. You're right, though, I'm not fit to become a man again. I'll be content just being Eva's pet. Sorry I bothered you."

"That's your trouble, Adamos. You give up too easily. That's how you got into this mess in the first place. You couldn't fight those dreadful feelings you harbored against Eva. There is good inside you, Adamos. Seek it. If you want something badly enough, you ought to fight for it."

"What's the use? I cannot fight you, Your Supreme Subjectness. A rabbit I am, a rabbit I deserve to be. Good evening ... and goodbye."

"I feel your pain, Adamos. And because I choose to believe you, I'll grant you your wish ..."

"... To remain a celibate rabbit?" interrupts Adamos.

"No ... to be a fully functioning and proper husband to Eva."

Adamos' eyes sparkle, his heart sings. "You ... you will? You will make me a man once again?"

"Yes. But slip up and a rabbit you will become again. Now, close your eyes."

"This I promise." Adamos bows his head. "My Eva will not see another day's labor. It is my place from now on to provide for her. Eva must pursue that which she desires."

"That is good, Adamos. But don't deprive her of the joy she feels doing voluntary work. Now, let's get on with the matter at hand. Close your eyes."

Adamos complies. Almost instantly, he feels a tingling sensation as if a bolt of electricity is surging through his body. Next, his rabbit body begins to expand vertically and horizontally. Adamos tries to open his eyes to see what is happening, but finds it impossible, as if a seal of blackness has been strapped across his eyes. When the expanding process finally stops, Adamos wriggles his fingers. They feel different, not at all like a rabbit's paws. He feels the same way when he wriggles his toes. A whiff of cool air touches his body and he shivers. *I'm stark naked!* He wishes he could voice his thoughts, but emotion forms a lump in his throat, constricting his voice.

"What are you waiting for?" asks the Creator. "Don't you wish to leave?"

Adamos shuffles uneasily. He swallows the lump in his throat and forces his lips to move. Compared to the rabbit's small mouth, his feels clumsy. Adamos reaches up and peels his lips apart with his fingers. Soundlessly he opens and shuts his mouth in an attempt to relax his jaws. When he dares speak, his voice sounds hoarse. "Lea ... lea ... leave? Like this?" he stammers awkwardly.

"Why? What's wrong now?"

Adamos touches his face and pulls his hands back as if he has touched red-hot coals. "You've left rabbit fur on my face for one."

"Not fur, Adamos, hair. You have quite a beard now."

"Well, aren't you going to remove it?"

"Deal with it, Adamos ... do something for yourself."

"I'm cold. Am I not naked?"

"So you are. And what a magnificent body!"

"And my ... my eyes? What ... what about them? Am I to return blind as well?"

"That I can fix."

Adamos feels a searing pain zip into his eyes and almost instantly exiting out the back of his head. His hands fly to caress the burning in his eyes. Soon the burning abates and Adamos cautiously open his eyes. He is astonished at the sharpness of his vision. He looks at himself, quickly covering his exposed private parts with his hands.

"I can't go back like this. What if people see me?"

"Not my worry, Adamos. Besides, I don't have a supply of clothing here, but this I want you to think about. Clothe yourself with humility. Now get going before I change my mind and return you to a rabbit ... or frog if you prefer."

Without another word, Adamos bolts from the shelter of the pine tree. He breaks off a leafy twig from an overhanging pine branch to cover his exposed body parts, and prays that the people of Edengardenia are all fast asleep. Using every available shadow from overhanging branches and tree trunks, Adamos picks his way carefully over jagged rocks, twigs, and small stones, his bare feet extra sensitive to the rough terrain. Tightness around his throat causes him to lift one hand. To his surprise, the bow is still there. "You forgot about the bow," he murmurs into the wind.

"Didn't," a musical whisper floats back to him.

Twenty

Meanwhile, at Neena's hut, Eva is frantically telling her sister about the state the rabbit was in when she left it. "You must come now, Neena. I think this time the rabbit is dying. It's only you who can save it … if it isn't too late already."

"I have no wish to help the stupid thing," protests Neena. "I'll be happy if it's dead this time, I tell you. You're better off without it, believe me."

"No, Neena. Don't say that, please. The rabbit means a lot to me now. I care deeply for it."

This surprises Neena. "But I thought you said you hated the dreadful thing."

"That was before. Come, Neena, no more questions."

"What made you change your mind, Eva? Tell me."

"It just happened, okay? Look, we're wasting precious time. Come. We must get back to the rabbit … now!"

Eva darts from Neena's hut, knowing she will follow. Beads of sweat gather across her brow and top lip. Her heart pounds louder with every anxious step she takes. Behind, she hears Neena grumbling.

At last they reach Eva's hut. Eva bursts through the door and quickly lights a lamp. She charges into the kitchen, to the spot where she left the ailing animal. "AOEEEEE!" she screams.

"What?" Neena rushes into the kitchen. "Is it dead?"

"It's gone. The rabbit's gone, Neena."

"Then it lives." Neena laughs, relief evident in her tone. "You needn't have worried so, Eva."

Eva ignores her sister and begins a frantic search for the rabbit. "Come, rabbit. Where are you? Don't hide, little darling." Eva calls in a singsong manner to the rabbit as she rushes from room to room. The rabbit does not appear. Eva lights several other lamps, shrinking the darkness to the far corners of the hut. Still the rabbit does not appear.

"I don't understand," says Eva, a lump forming in her throat. "How can the rabbit just disappear?"

"Perhaps it followed you when you came to get me," offers Neena kindly. Privately, though, she thinks: *So, Adamos, you've done a runner again!*

"Perhaps you are right, Neena. Perhaps it did follow me out the door. Then we must go out and search for it. The poor thing has never been outside this hut since the day I fetched it from the mountain. Come, Neena, we must comb every scrap of land and carrot patch for my beloved Chubby."

The women burst out of the hut leaving the door ajar. Adamos barely has time to dart behind a row of hibiscus bushes. "That was close." From a gap in his bushy shelter, Adamos peers at the women. "They are in a panic. Of course! They can't find the rabbit."

When the women rush behind the hut, Adamos relaxes. But seeing Eva sends shivers spiraling down his spine. "Oh my love!" He takes deep breaths hoping to stem the throbbing in his loin. He wraps his arms around his body. The leafy twig he is holding to shield his private parts drops to the ground. Adamos makes no attempt to retrieve it. Perhaps this is the time to clothe himself with humility.

The women re-emerge from behind the hut. When they charge down the path, stopping every so often to thrash the grass and call to the lost rabbit, Adamos holds his breath, for fear he will be discovered.

"We must take our search along the road to your hut, Neena," he hears Eva say. "Perhaps the rabbit could have followed me there."

"Or it might be lying dead at the bottom of the stream," says Neena.

"Don't say that. If the rabbit came outdoors it was when I charged out to get you. It's probably tangled up in shrub along the path to your hut."

Adamos releases his breath when the women zip past. "I'd better get into the hut, have a cold bath, and put some clothes on before they return," chatters Adamos, feeling chilly even though there is no wind. "Except the only clothes I have lie at the bottom of my cage … and they smell like rabbit." His mind is in turmoil. "And how am I going to explain my sudden reappearance to Eva when she sees me?"

Adamos reaches up to scratch an itchy spot behind his right ear and his finger connects with the earring Eva had attached to his ear when he was a rabbit. "Oh, no!" He tries to yank it off, but almost rips his earlobe. "What am I to do now?"

Poor Adamos! Being naked is one thing … reappearing as a slimmer Adamos is another thing … but to reappear wearing an earring and a pink bow! Well, that will take some explaining. "What will Eva think when she finds out the rabbit and I are one and the same? Will she even care that I, her husband, have returned? Will she overcome the shock that her husband was once a rabbit?" Adamos sighs. Perhaps he should not return to the hut at all.

With a heavy heart, Adamos detaches himself from the hibiscus bush, intending to return to the mountain, but his feet and body take on a will of their own and propel him down the path leading to the hut. Offering no resistance, Adamos allows his legs to take him inside the hut. He closes the door behind him. The hut is ablaze with lamplight.

The first thing Adamos sees is a pile of yellow nuggets on the table where his rabbit cage once stood. His jaw drops open. The pile of nuggets is equivalent to the pile he had stolen from Eva. "Thank you, Creator, for doing this splendid deed."

In the lamplight, Adamos examines his body. Another surprise awaits—his once flabby and wrinkled skin is tight and young. Strong muscles form ripples where his abdomen once protruded. He stretches out his arms and is equally amazed at the bulging biceps. He feels young and full of vigor again, as if he has the body of a thirty-year-old.

Remembering Eva keeps a bucket of water outside the back door, Adamos uses it to wash himself. There are no clothes for him to wear, so he grabs a woven blanket and drapes it loosely around his waist, leaving his muscular chest exposed. He remembers that Eva has kept his bar of wild berry and tallow soap, and shaving knife. Grabbing the soap, Adamos quickly lathers his face and with the knife swiftly removes the growth of hair from his face. He combs his fingers through his shoulder length hair. He will not cut it. He unravels a short length of string from the blanket and uses it to tie his hair into a ponytail. Next, he blows out all but two lamps. The semi-darkness will conceal him for a time. Adamos paces back and forth across the main room floor, his thoughts searching for ways to explain his sudden reappearance … as well as his changed physique.

The thumping feet and muffled voices of the women approaching send Adamos scurrying into the kitchen, still unsure of what his next move should be.

"Please, Great Creator, at least remove the bow." Adamos clears the huskiness from his throat.

His request is granted. The bow loosens and floats to the ground. Adamos kicks it under the table; only then did he remember the spot behind Eva's jars of herbs and tea leaves, where he toileted when he was a rabbit. He stares at the spot; his immediate thought to remove the evidence. He must act quickly, but his legs seem rooted to the ground.

Twenty-one

Eva opens the door and half steps into the hut. She sucks in her breath. "Neena," she whispers, backing out and pulling the door shut, "something is wrong." A queer shiver runs up and down her spine.

"Of course, silly. We've lost the rabbit, but we already know that."

"No, Neena, it's the lamps ... only two burning in the hut. Several were lit when we raced out in search of the rabbit. And this door ... it was shut. I don't remember shutting it when we raced from the hut, unless you did. Did you?"

Neena shakes her head from side to side, her eyes wide with concern. "It's the wind that closed the door, Eva," she stammers nervously. "It's the wind that blew the lamps out ... before it blew the door shut; it's the wind that ...."

"Don't talk crazy, Neena. There's no wind. Look, nothing moves, not even the dry leaves on the path. No, Neena, something is wrong. Something or someone is hiding, waiting for us in there. But why?"

"What should we do, Eva?" Neena whispers.

"We must go in." Eva bites down on her bottom lip, her face determined. "There are two of us. Pick up a stone, Neena, a big one. We'll bash the skull of whoever or whatever is hiding in there."

The women each pick up a large stone. Taking a deep breath, Eva heaves her shoulder against the door. It flies open and she stumbles in.

Recovering her equilibrium, Eva spies the glow from the pile of nuggets on the table. Startled, she sucks in a deep breath. "Neena." A mere whisper escapes her lips. She clears her throat. "Neena, look, the nuggets have been returned." Eva sniffs the air. "And I can smell Adamos' wild berry and tallow soap."

"What? But that can't be. Does it mean ... that Adamos ... " Neena picks up one of the lit lamps.

The sound of pots clattering to the ground sends the sisters crashing into each other in their haste to make a speedy exit. The stones spill out of their hands. They scramble to recover them. Then, gathering their composure, Eva and Neena edge cautiously towards the kitchen instead; the jagged stones dig painfully into the palms of their hands. The lamplight illuminates the tiny kitchen.

Eva sucks in her breath and her eyes widen when she sees a younger version of Adamos holding a pot in one hand. A blanket wrapped loosely around his waist conceals his lower body leaving his upper body exposed. *It is as it was in my dream*, thinks Eva, feeling confused.

"Adamos?" she calls softly. "How can this be?"

Adamos and Eva stare at each other. Adamos feels the corners of his mouth begin to twitch as if he were still a rabbit. Eva shakes her head. "No. You're not Adamos. He's fat and old and almost bald. He's gone. Who are you? What are you doing here … dressed like that?"

Eva rambles on nervously, as if words alone will make the apparition disappear. "How dare you expose yourself so? How dare you use Adamos' soap?" Then spying the pink bow under the table, Eva becomes livid. "The rabbit! What have you done with it?" She picks up the bow and dangles it in front of Adamos. "You killed the rabbit, didn't you … hoping to make rabbit stew!"

"But it is really I, my love. I have returned," stammers Adamos, struggling to control the tremor in his voice and the twitch at the corners of his mouth.

"Returned?" Eva is lost for words.

"Have you now?" Neena jumps in, poking her head above Eva's shoulder. "But how did you change back from being a …."

"Yes," Adamos answers before Neena has a chance to say 'rabbit.' "I have returned."

"At least you were honest enough to return Eva's nuggets." Neena narrows her eyes, studying the man.

"Well … I … yes, I suppose I am."

Even though the muscular man before her has blue-green eyes

like Adamos, Eva is still unconvinced he is really Adamos as he was many years ago. Losing weight is one thing, but retarding the aging process? "No, don't believe a word this imposter says," Eva bursts out, pushing Neena aside. "He is not Adamos. He cannot be. If he will not tell us the truth, then perhaps a good pounding will make him." Eva hoists the stone above her head, readying to bring it crashing down on Adamos' skull.

Adamos pulls back, shocked at Eva's aggression. He somehow manages to stop his mouth twitching. "Don't, my love, please."

Seeing the hurt in Adamos' eyes, Neena feels an instant empathy for him. The years of hatred between them melt away like fat in a hot pan. "Stop, Eva." Neena scrambles to prevent the downward motion of her sister's arm.

"Why should I?" asks Eva, trying to tug her arm away from Neena.

"It is you who is wrong." Neena clears her throat. "Adamos has come back to you and he has returned the nuggets too."

"Then you are as mad as this imposter who claims to be my Adamos," declares Eva angrily, lifting her arm again.

"What if I can prove it?" asks Neena, remembering the earring, which she hopes Adamos is still wearing.

"How? What do you know about Adamos that I don't know?" Eva's anger spikes dangerously.

"No, Neena, please … don't make me …" begs Adamos, intuitively knowing what she is asking. "Perhaps it is wrong for me to come back."

"You know her name?" Eva is confused. "Neena, what is this? What have you done? Why are you and this man conspiring to deceive me?" Feeling suddenly betrayed, Eva backs away from her sister.

"Turn your head, Adamos," pleads Neena. "Turn so she can see the proof. Do it, Adamos. Do it, please. Your future depends on it."

Adamos can resist no longer. Neena is right. He must reveal the earring, which Eva had placed in his ear—whatever the consequences. "Very well." Adamos' voice is soft; his eyes burn into

Eva's. Slowly he turns his head to the left, bringing the earring on his right ear into full view.

Eva gasps. Her suddenly weakened knee-joints fail to support her. She grabs the wall to steady herself. Eva's chin begins to tremble. "But … that is the earring I attached to the rabbit's ear …!"

Eva's hand flies to her mouth, stifling the scream, as full realization of the situation dawns. She shakes her head in disbelief. "No. No. I won't believe any of this. Please, Neena, please tell me this is a cruel joke. Tell me for the last time this man isn't my Adamos. Tell me the rabbit wasn't really Adamos."

There is no other way, thinks Neena. No matter how cruel it seems, she must confess now. "I knew for a long time, Eva, that the rabbit was Adamos … we have been communicating. I'm sorry, Eva … for not telling you."

"You what? He wasn't with …" Eva's lips quiver, the tone of her voice mirrors her disbelief; her eyes sting. Not only has Adamos betrayed her, but now her precious sister has too. This new revelation is too much. Eva bursts into tears, her body trembling with each heartbreaking sob.

Adamos rushes to her. "Don't cry, my love, please. I'm so sorry I hurt you these past years." His tone is apologetic, but full of sincerity. "The Creator of all that is has made me see sense … when He turned me into a rabbit."

"The Creator of all that is? What is this you say, Adamos?" Eva splutters.

"You call it the Tree of Solitude, Eva, but it is more. It is the Creator. You once asked me how Edengardenia came to be. I admit I didn't know the answer then, but I do now. The Great Pine … this island … you … me …. the Creator has made everything. He is everywhere, Eva, everywhere. Yes, my love, the Creator changed me into a rabbit … the rabbit you blindfolded. I was that rabbit you so hated at first but came to love. Ten lost years have been restored to me and I must use them to correct the errors of my ways. Yes, my sweet, I no longer see with blind eyes. I will love and respect you, as I should have done before. The Creator has granted me a second chance, my love. I must tell our people about the Creator. Yes … you must sing for me, my sweet, sing all day long. Sing until the moon turns green." Adamos gushes, unable to control his raging emotions. "Let me comfort you, my love, please. Say you forgive me."

Adamos wraps his muscular arms tightly around Eva, cradling her against his bare chest. Eva offers no resistance this time. She lets her head fall heavily against Adamos' strong chest. Streams of water spill from her eyes.

"My love, I have been such a selfish fool," Adamos whispers hoarsely, tilting her head upwards with his index finger, his thumb gently caressing her chin. Adamos' emotions peek and with a groan, he lowers his head claiming the wet softness of his wife's lips. The blanket slides slowly down Adamos' lean body. "I promise not to eat all the meat in future," he whispers hoarsely between kisses.

My Adamos is back, all right, thinks Eva. *He always says the most unromantic things at the wrong time.*

"My sweet, sweet Eva," Adamos groans, struggling to control the energy surging through his body, "from now on I will be the one to work, do repairs … you, my love, must do the things you enjoy, whatever they may be."

Eva moans softly. Already she is beginning to like this new Adamos … if it really is Adamos!

Recognizing the need for Adamos and Eva to be alone, Neena slips out of the kitchen and out of the hut. A contented smile spreads across her lips. There is a fair bit of explaining to do. She doubts whether that will be done anytime soon!

Once outside, Neena stops and stares at the mountain. Tiny white lights seem to dance around its peak. "You too are delighted, Creator of all that is," she whispers. "You are the author of my sister's happiness. Thank you. If there's anyone who deserves to be happy right now, it's her."

As if hearing Neena's every word, the lights dance faster, then funneling like a tornado, corkscrew down the center of the peak.

"This is most remarkable," whispers Neena, feeling honored to witness such magnificence. "Whether the taking of the rib has affected man or not, there is hope for him to renew his mind."

With one last look at Eva's hut, Neena turns and heads for her own home, her heart full to overflowing. "Now, I'm ready to find a husband … a perfect husband like the new Adamos."

Neena feels as if she has been reborn. Her heart lurches and she feels as if a heavy iron bolt has drawn back, sending a surge of deep emotion gushing to the surface. Then a soft whispery voice drifts into her hearing: "But remember, Neena … there's no such thing as a *perfect* husband."

Technically, this is where the story should end, but ….

Twenty-two

Even though Eva feels joy at Adamos' return, and great relief that he never was with that other woman, she is still unconvinced it is he. One look at him, blissfully asleep with a smile on his face, prompts her into action. She creeps out of bed and puts on her clothes. She eases out of the hut. The moon provides enough light to guide her steps as she hurries up the path to the mountain. Once she has reached the Great Pine, she sits upon the stump. She gathers her thoughts and allows her breathing to normalize.

"Eva? Why are you here before sunrise? Is everything all right?"

"That I do not know, Great Creator ... may I call you that?"

"Yes, you may, Eva. But how did you deduce this information?"

"You see, there is a man in my hut who claims to be the new Adamos ... it is he who told me this thing," replies Eva. "And he told me another thing which I don't understand."

"What might that be, Eva?"

"He said you are everywhere."

"And he is right, Eva. I am ... everywhere."

"But how can that be?"

"I just am. Let that be sufficient, Eva ... for now."

Eva is silent for a time. She laces her fingers together.

"Don't you like the *new* Adamos, Eva?" asks the Creator.

"Even if he really is Adamos, Great Creator, how do I know he has changed for the better?"

"Time will tell," replies the Creator.

"I have an idea, Great Creator. Will you change me into a crow? That way I can observe Adamos to see if he really has changed his ways."

"A crow, Eva?"

"Yes," Eva replies with confidence. "Adamos hates them."

"It isn't necessary for you to be such, Eva. The Adamos you see has indeed changed. Believe it in your heart."

"But …" Eva is still doubtful.

"Do not doubt, Eva. Return to Adamos. A crow, which I have sent, sits in the tree outside your hut. Its squawk is loud and irritating. The old Adamos would throw a stone at the bird to chase it away, but the new Adamos will not. When he says to you, 'I have befriended a crow, Eva. I will have to give it squawking lessons, though,' then you must release all doubt and believe what I've told you."

"I will. Thank you, Great Creator."

Meanwhile, back at the hut, Adamos stirs. His ears attune to the sweet chirping of the birds, but the squawking of one bird stirs his memories. "You sing like my wife … used to," he corrects himself. He reaches out to embrace Eva and is surprised to find she is not beside him.

"Ah, my Eva is up early. I must go to her."

Adamos scrambles out of bed, wondering why no lamps burn. "Eva," he calls softly, "are you listening to the birds? They are happy that I have returned." He lights a lamp and carries it to the kitchen. "Eva …! Where are you?"

Adamos searches the entire hut, but does not find Eva. "She must have gone to the mountain," Adamos concludes.

He will make Eva breakfast—scrambled seagull's eggs, seasoned with wild herbs, served on flatbread. She will like that. Wrapping a blanket around him, for he still has no clothes, he hurries out of the hut. He will search the rocks on the beach where the gulls lay their eggs. It is still quite dark. No one will see him.

As Adamos walks past the tree where the crow is perched, he hears the loud squawk again and looks up for the offending bird. Because it is dark, he does not see the black bird, except for its bright eyes.

"You need squawking lessons, my friend," says Adamos with politeness, "if you're to squawk to the world each morning. But I mustn't tarry, for I must seek gulls eggs for my Eva. She's sure to be hungry when she returns from the mountain. Keep squawking, though, you're bound to improve. If you're lucky, I'll even give you squawking lessons."

Adamos walks on and stops. Returning to the bird, he says, "You must take a deep breath before you squawk. Practice while I'm gone and when I return I will tell you if you have improved."

Adamos picks his way cautiously along the sandy path to the beach. Damp sand clings to his feet and seep between his toes. Adamos remembers one particular rock near the edge of the water, where seagulls like to lay their eggs, and hurries towards it. He is in luck. He finds three eggs, still warm, perhaps freshly hatched. He gently gathers the eggs, softly whispering his apologies to the absent seagull for robbing her of her future offspring. He retraces his steps to the hut, his heart full of joy, his thoughts only of Eva.

The crow is still squawking as Adamos walks past the tree. He stops briefly. "You are improving, bird." He chuckles. "But I mustn't dilly-dally. My Eva will soon return and I must have breakfast ready for her. You don't know how to make flatbread, do you, crow?"

It is some time before Eva returns. Although the seagull's eggs and flatbread are stone cold now, Adamos is not angry. He rushes to the door.

"Good morning, my love." He takes Eva into his arms for a brief hug and peck on her cheek.

"Good morning, Ad ... Adamos," Eva stutters. She sniffs the air. "I smell seagull's eggs and flatbread? Have you ...?"

"Yes, my love, I made you breakfast."

"But ... seagull's eggs? How ...?"

"I went to the rocks, my love."

Just then, the crow squawks. This makes Adamos laugh. "I have befriended a crow, Eva. I will have to give it squawking lessons, though."

At hearing these words, Eva remembers what the Creator has said. She bursts into tears. "Oh, Adamos ... it is really you."

Still laughing, Adamos tightens his arms around Eva. "Of course it is I, my love. But do you cry because I have decided to give the crow squawking lessons? Or is it because I actually prepared breakfast?" he teases.

"I'm sorry for the dreadful things I said when ...."

"Sssssh, my love! Let the past remain in the past. We have a new beginning. I intend to make the most of it."

Eva laughs then, and allows Adamos to wipe away her tears with his thumb. This was a gentler Adamos. The old Adamos would have yelled at her to stop the waterworks, spew insults at her for not having breakfast ready, and throw rocks at the crow for being so noisy.

"I will come with you to the mountain tomorrow, my sweet," whispers Adamos, brushing his lips softy against Eva's, "... and all the tomorrows after that."

Eva sighs deeply. It has been a long time since she felt so happy and secure, so feminine and appreciated.

Epilogue

He who finds a wife, finds a good thing!

Printed in the United States
24181LVS00001B/64

9 781413 757606